Riley's RESCUE

Riley's RESCUE

BY

LEXI POST

RILEY'S RESCUE
Last Chance Series, Book 6

By Lexi Post

Army veteran, Riley O'Hare, is a loner for a reason—it's safe, and it keeps her sane. After calling animal welfare on her last boss, she accepted the position of a ranch hand for the Last Chance Ranch. But things have become almost too comfortable. The only reason she's stayed so long is she works alone…a lot.

Garrett Walker is a former Hot Shot, part of a special breed of firefighters who battle wildfires. At loose ends, he becomes the rescue horse hauler for Last Chance Ranch. When he meets the tough, distant Riley, he finds his usual aptitude for sizing up a person is completely useless. Either she's as odd as she appears or her layers run deep.

It's only after they spend time in close proximity in an abandoned copper mine that he uncovers more about her, inadvertently revealing his own weakness. A need to keep her in his life grows too strong to ignore. Their occupational scars may be impossible to overcome, but he was a Hot Shot for a reason. Jumping into fires has been his specialty…and his downfall.

For updates, sneak peeks, and special prizes, sign up to receive the latest news from Lexi http://bit.ly/LexiUpdate

Acknowledgments

For Bob Fabich, Sr., my own firefighter who sees me as an equal in every way. And for my sister Paige Wood, who always makes time for my stories.

I had a lot of help with this book. Pamela Reveal came up with Riley's last name. Thank you, Pamela. Thank you to Rita Cassidy-Kern Clements for coming up with the perfect name for the mine.

In addition, I need to thank Linda Herold and Michelle Hedgcock for being loyal readers who not only read my books, but my meandering newsletter as well. Love your comments ladies. You're the best!

A special thank you to Marie Patrick, who never lets me forget that I'm a storyteller.

This story is dedicated to Schatzie, Marie's wonderful German Shepherd who loved her unconditionally. A unique dog that will never be forgotten.

And I can't close without saying thank you to Lisa Fishback, Denise Hendrickson, KC, and Michelle Hedgcock for their time helping me whip this book into shape.

Author's Note

Riley's Rescue was inspired by Bret Harte's short story, "High-Water Mark." It is a story about a young woman and her child living in a cabin on a river that flowed into a bay. Her husband leaves for his job, which is to work for a lumber company. That night, a storm comes up that is particularly strong. The water rises, and she goes through a harrowing experience as she takes her sickly baby and jumps onto a large tree that has swept against the cabin just before the cabin falls into the swirling waters. In the pitch black, she judges her position based on sounds and the taste of the water, thereby knowing when she reaches the bay. Eventually, she sees the light of the light house, and this is where the great tree snags on the bottom, halting its progress. She and her baby are rescued by two Native American women. Her husband, upon his return, is anxious he has lost her, but finds her when the tide goes out. He uses the tree to build a new cabin farther up the river above the high-water mark.

But what if the woman had to go through a similar experience again, only this time with someone at her side? Would that make it easier or would the experience drive her beyond hope or sanity? And how could he be of any help, when he doesn't know what she'd actually experienced the first time? Could love truly overcome a second unbearable trauma?

Chapter One

Riley O'Hare stepped out onto the porch of the two-story ranch house of Last Chance Ranch and halted, the screen door still in her hand. "Well, shit."

Letting the door slam behind her, she jogged down the three steps to the hard-packed Arizona dirt and ran for the south corral. Cyclone, their resident Clydesdale, and technically Dr. Jenna's horse, ran circles around the enclosure.

Looking over her shoulder, she scanned the area in front of the house. Only her pick-up truck sat there of the more than four that usually graced the yard. In her peripheral vision, she noticed dust on the dirt road to the ranch, but didn't have time to focus.

It better be Cole. He was supposed to take Cyclone to the abandoned copper mine to pull out some fallen timbers. She'd flatly refused to go anywhere near the decrepit mine, so he'd agreed to do it. It was the perfect chore for Cyclone. If the big horse wasn't given work to do at least every third day, he started breaking things. And she was the one who had to fix them.

Jumping onto the lower rail of the fencing, she waved her arm. "Cyclone! Come here, boy!" She just needed to break up his windup. From what she'd learned, he'd been well-named. The running in circles behavior was the precursor to major damage.

She tried again. "Cyclone!" Putting two fingers to her mouth, she let out a shrill whistle.

The Clydesdale slowed, bouncing his head once and looking at her.

"Come here, boy. I've got work for you."

As if he knew she lied, he started to pick up the pace.

"Well, crap." Jumping off the rail, she made a beeline for the barn. There had to be something in there for Cyclone to pull. Rounding the corner of the open barn doors, she grinned. "Perfect." Jumping onto the four-wheeler, she turned the key they always left in it and drove out of the barn and straight for the corral.

A truck with a horse trailer pulled to a stop in front of the house. Hoping Manuel could handle the new horse and whatever its issues were until she could get Cyclone settled, she stopped the ATV and jumped off.

Unfortunately, Cyclone had stopped, too.

"No, Cyclone!" She brought her fingers to her lips once again, but she was too late. The big horse's back legs lifted and he smashed the top rail of the corral. Wood flew everywhere, and she ducked. Then before the horse could gear-up for another kick, she climbed up on the fence post closest to him and jumped.

Grasping his mane, she cooed as he walked sideways. "Come on boy, I've got some work for—"

A strong arm grabbed her around the waist from behind and pulled her off to the side.

Not expecting that, she lost her grip on Cyclone and her full weight fell onto the person beneath her. They both went toppling to the ground inside the enclosure.

She rolled out of his grasp and jumped to her feet, more worried about the horse than the stranger lying on the ground inside the corral. Spotting Cyclone starting his circle run again, she brushed off her jeans before glaring at the cowboy now rising to his feet. "What the hell do you think you're doing?"

Striding past him, she climbed over the corral fence and hopped back on the four-wheeler.

"What am I doing? I'm saving your neck."

She barely spared him a glance as he picked up his cowboy hat and ran for the fence himself as Cyclone headed directly for him.

"If you want to help go get the collar harness hanging on the hook inside the barn while I keep him from jumping the fence."

Not caring if the dark-haired stranger bothered to listen to her or not, she turned the machine on and drove it parallel to the broken fence to fill the gap. The last thing she needed was a runaway Cyclone.

Not sure what the horse would do next, she jumped off and watched as he approached. He trotted by as if the four-wheeler was another part of the corral.

Figuring she had about thirty seconds before Cyclone came around again, she turned her attention to the cowboy who approached, harness in hand. She pointed to the horse trailer. "Is the horse in there okay for a few more minutes?"

At his nod, she waved toward the ATV. "Good. Do you think you can hook that up to the ATV?"

His brow furrowed. "I just saw you drive it. Why would you need to tow it?"

Cyclone was coming around again. Either she needed to get back on his back or let him out. Otherwise, there'd be two fence rails to repair. "Just tell me, can you do it?" Irritation colored her tone, but she didn't have time for pleasantries. Where the hell was Manny anyway?

The cowboy threw her a scowl before moving to the ATV.

She climbed on the fence. Maybe if she could interrupt the big horse's stride, it might take him a bit to build up steam again. Jumping to the ground, she ran out in front of him, waving her arms. "Whoa, Cyclone!"

The Clydesdale swerved in midstride, cutting short his circle.

Just great. Turning back to the cowboy, she found him staring at her his eyes appearing almost silver. For shit's sake. "Is it hooked?"

"Are you trying to get yourself killed?" He dropped the harness and stalked to the fence.

She met him there. "No, I'm trying to keep this big boy from destroying the corral." She climbed over the fence and picked up the harness then dropped it on the handle bars of the machine. "Open the gate." She didn't wait to see if he would help. She just put the ATV in gear.

Come on, Cyclone, skip the break in the fence and get to work.

The cowboy opened the gate, so she drove the machine into the corral. Turning off the engine, she jumped to the ground and rattled the harness just as Cyclone approached the opening with the broken rail.

His ears perked up as he slowed, coming to a stop next to her. "Good boy. You ready to work?"

The Clydesdale's big brown eyes followed her as she started to lift the heavy harness onto him. When the weight was lessened, she nodded to the cowboy who lifted the other half onto the big brute. Once she had Cyclone hitched, she strode to the ATV and sat in the seat, hoping the harness would hold. Leaving the engine off, she shifted the machine into neutral. "Okay, Cyclone. Let's bring this baby to Cole's house." Clicking her tongue, she grabbed the handles wrapped in reins and the horse started to walk.

When the horse exited the corral, towing the ATV with her on it, she finally gave the cowboy her attention as he closed the gate behind her. Nice ass, not uncommon among the cowboys she'd worked with. He was clean shaven, broad at the shoulders and slender at the hips. He wore a long sleeve shirt, which she'd find stifling in the dry heat, though many landscapers did that. She assumed it was to avoid burning from the brutal Arizona sun.

He came up next to her as Cyclone plodded along. "So, what's this? Some kind of therapy?"

His eyes were actually a blue-grey and at the moment filled with curiosity as opposed to censure, which is what she would have expected from a stranger watching her over the last twenty minutes. Now that she had a good look at him, he reminded her of some of her military buddies before they'd all headed to the Middle East and changed. He had less swagger than the typical cowboy and a more commanding presence, but he was just as handsome as the rest at Last Chance. What was it, a prerequisite to work there?

She forced her attention back to his question. "Not exactly therapy. Cyclone likes to work, which means he likes to pull heavy objects. If he's left to his own devices for more than three days, he lives up to his name." She hooked her thumb over her shoulder. "And I'm the one left with the repairs."

He glanced back toward the broken fence of the corral before facing forward again. "Cole told me when he offered me the job that there would be some odd personalities." He chuckled. "I thought he meant the ranch hands."

She smothered a smirk. There were definitely some interesting human personalities on Last Chance, but the horses beat them out. "Where's Manuel?"

The cowboy grinned, and when he did his straight white

teeth showed, making him appear very relaxed. "Grandson due any day and his daughter offered him and his wife to move onto their ranch in New Mexico. Nothing stronger than family ties."

Right. Family ties. In her family, those ties had been as likely to hang her as help her. "I'm Riley O'Hare. I do a bit of everything around here. To look at this place right now, you'd never know there are actually eight others involved with this rescue operation."

He reached over as he walked along next to her. "I'm Garrett Walker. I'll be the one bringing you horses."

She shook, his grip firm, not crushing, but the rough texture of the skin on the back of his right hand told her he had some serious scars. "Speaking of horses, what's the story with that one?" She nodded toward the trailer in front of them before she directed Cyclone to turn right down the dirt road that would take them to Cole's house.

"Just old. If you can stop Cyclone here for a moment, I'll take her out and walk with you. She'd probably like to stretch her legs."

She pulled on the reins for her answer.

Garrett strode over to the trailer and unlocked the back. Yup, definitely a more military bearing. That had to be why she felt comfortable with him. She hadn't been with fellow veterans in two years. On one hand, getting together with her former unit members was like old home week, but it always brought back bad memories, so she'd avoided the last two "get-togethers."

She watched the new hauler's moves. He was confident in his actions and comfortable around the horse. Probably grew up with horses. Yet when he'd leaned in to shake hands, she caught a scent of aftershave with an almost clove-like scent. Most of the cowboy's she'd run to when all cleaned up smelled more like soap or fresh linen. She liked the richer smell Garrett wore.

He walked a pretty buckskin quarter horse out of the trailer toward her. Yeah, totally confident and seriously had the face of an actor, more of a Captain America look than a GI Joe.

At the new horse's presence, Cyclone's head swiveled bringing her focus back to him. "Give her a nice welcome, boy, but don't be getting any ideas." Not that she needed to worry. Cyclone had the weirdest crush on Tiny Dancer, who was the frailest mare on the ranch.

He brought the horse over and allowed Cyclone and her to get acquainted.

"What's her name?"

"Lady, though I was told the old man who owned her started calling her Old Lady about seven years ago."

Old Lady? "Was that because Lady is getting older or because the owner was from the seventies?"

Garrett chuckled.

The sound reminded her of the rest of the men on Last Chance. They were always in a good mood. She found that seriously strange. Garrett was also just as good-looking and appeared to have the typical cowboy manners. Not bad overall.

"It was because Lady here is twenty-two, but from what I've seen, she's in very good health for her age."

From what she could see, she agreed, but she'd have Dr. Jenna come over and do her usual "welcome to Last Chance" physical.

Garrett clicked his tongue and Lady started to walk.

She didn't need to encourage Cyclone. The big horse started pulling her as soon as Lady moved beyond him. Typical male. Just couldn't stand to walk a few paces behind a woman. She squelched her attitude. "So why is Lady here?"

"Her owner died." Garrett spoke over his shoulder because Lady was determined to remain in the lead.

"The family doesn't want to keep her or sell her?" It was rare that they received horses who were simply old. To her, they didn't really qualify as rescues. Most of the horses that came to Last Chance were like Nizhoni and Phoenix, the ones she'd been able to get away from her boss at the time.

Cyclone was moving along at a good clip now, determined to keep abreast of Lady. Garrett walked next to the ATV. "There's two more coming. I'll be bringing them by in another day or two. No one in the family has the property to take them on, which from what I saw would have been their first choice. They seem to care for these horses as much as their grandfather. In fact, one of them will be coming here to stay for a few days to make sure this is the right place for them to live out their lives."

Now that was a first. "I would think knowing this is a rescue ranch would be enough."

Garrett lost his easy-going smile. "It should be, but the youngest grandson was the closest to the old man and is very particular about how they're cared for. I think it's his way of dealing with his grief. He actually made me read a two-page write-up on how to transport them."

She groaned. She'd had by-the-book men under her command, and they just didn't realize that sometimes the "book" went up in flames. There was no way this would be good. "Are you saying this young man is coming here to make us all read policies and procedures on how to care for these horses?"

If that was the case, she would make herself scarce for a couple days. No young punk was going to tell her how to care for horses. She'd grown up with horses, even sleeping with them in the barn she worked in when she couldn't stand to be home.

"I'm not sure what he has planned. I feel for him. It's hard losing someone you're close to."

At his serious tone, she glanced at him. Had he experienced

what she had? The idea brought both sympathy and defenses. The only reason she was functioning normally now was because she wasn't around others who'd had her experience. Luckily, he was just the horse hauler.

Lady pulled ahead again, so she didn't have to make more conversation, which was just as well. She needed to figure out what Cole might have in his barn that Cyclone could haul back to the main house. She didn't care what it was because if Cole had done what he'd said he was going to do, she wouldn't be on an ATV right now being pulled by a horse for no reason whatsoever.

Most likely he'd been called into a fire early in the morning. Ever since he'd made Captain, his hours were less regulated, as his wife Lacey had mentioned more than once. He was also less present regarding the operations of the ranch. She'd thought about asking to be the manager, but she didn't want that kind of permanence. She'd already stayed at Last Chance longer than usual. There was something about the place that let her be herself, but that was dangerous. She couldn't afford to feel close to anyone.

"Have you worked for Cole long?" Garrett had managed to bring Lady even with Cyclone again.

"Depends on your perspective. For me, it's been a long time." She slowed Cyclone as they reached the barn at Cole's. The new home and barn were less than a mile away, so Cyclone wouldn't be happy if there was nothing more to haul. After jumping off the ATV, she strode into the barn.

Garrett hitched Lady to the new corral fence then made to follow her.

She stopped him. "Wait, let me see if there's anything in here the big guy can haul. Angel is afraid of men, so if there's no reason for you to come inside, I'd rather not stress her."

"Angel? She's afraid of men? Why?"

She swallowed a flippant remark. The cowboy had just been hired, of course he wouldn't know. "Angel is Lacey's horse. She's skittish even around women, but she was abused by a man."

Garrett's low whistle made it clear he understood, and she entered the cooler space.

She ignored Samson, Cole's black quarter horse while giving Angel her space, and looked into each stall and the tack area. The new barn was as clean as a boot camp polished belt buckle. Shit. Except for a few haybales, there was nothing for Cyclone to pull. Now what? She couldn't ask the horse to drag her around on the ATV all day.

Chapter Two

G arrett turned away from the open barn and strolled around the corner. Riley O'Hare had more bristle on her than a prickly pear cactus. Everything about her screamed "keep your distance" and from the look of her arms in her black tank, he had a feeling she could force the issue if she wanted to.

She reminded him of the one woman on his old team, only Riley's voice was deeper with a rasp quality that was hard to ignore. Was that why Riley was the way she was, because she was the only female ranch hand? It was obvious she knew horses. After dragging her off the Clydesdale when he'd arrived, he'd got the message that his help wasn't wanted. Or rather, not in the way his instincts told him to help. Still, it had taken every ounce of willpower not to push her out of the way as Cyclone galloped for her.

His brain told him she knew what the horse was capable of, but his natural reaction was to protect a woman, and despite her roughness, she was definitely that. Her full cheeks were the perfect setting for brown eyes so dark they appeared black. Her nose turned up just a bit, and that combined with her full lips gave her a more feminine look than he'd guess she appreciated.

She wasn't slender but neither was she curvy. She had a robustness that wouldn't get swept away in the next haboob with a slight curve between waist and hips and more on her chest. Boyish wouldn't describe her, though for some reason he had a feeling she'd prefer that description. Her thick, straight, red hair though was like a warning beacon to keep his distance.

Turning the corner to the back of the barn, he halted. A pile of brand-new lumber was stacked neatly as if just delivered. He strolled closer. Maybe brand new wasn't quite the word. Grass had grown up between the stacks telling him it had been there at least a week.

"You still here?" At the sound of her voice, he strode back the way he'd come.

"I'm here. Just wandering."

She hooked her thumb over her shoulder. "There's nothing in there I can use. I'll have to have him pull me back on the ATV. Hopefully, that will appease him long enough for me to get Lady settled in."

"There's a couple stacks of lumber behind the barn. Would that work?"

"What?"

She strode past him, the scent of ginger spice catching him off guard. He didn't take her for the baking type. More intrigued, he crossed his arms and waited for her to return.

"You've got to be kidding!" Her exclamation was loud enough that even Lady perked up her ears. It didn't take long for Riley to reappear. "That lumber was delivered a couple weeks back for Cole's new deck. He was in a damn hurry for me to get Cyclone to drag it down here."

He didn't say anything. He just waited to see what she'd do next.

A slow smile spread across her face, transforming it into something much softer and approachable, despite the sly grin. "Guess Cyclone will just have to bring it back."

Her statement brought his brain back on track. "Whoa, do you think Cole will appreciate that?" The man was her boss, after all. His, too, technically.

She shrugged. "Not my problem. If he'd taken Cyclone out to the mine this morning or at least called someone else to, I wouldn't be in this position. I still have a fence rail to fix in addition to everything else on my list. That means if Cyclone wants to lug lumber back to the main house, then that's what I have to do. I don't have all day to cater to his whims."

Without asking for help, she unhitched the harness from the ATV and guided Cyclone to the back of the barn.

He didn't move, not sure how well that was going to go over with Cole. Cole was an old friend. They'd both earned their associates in Fire Science at the community college before landing jobs in different parts of the state. Cole had always been half cowboy and half firefighter. That's why they'd rubbed along well.

As if she'd forgotten he was there, Riley led Cyclone past the barn and onto the dirt road back to the main house, the lumber still strapped together as it had arrived. Yes, she was definitely different. He walked over to where Lady eyed Cyclone, obviously not happy that he had a head start on her.

He patted the mare's side. "Don't worry, we'll catch up to them." Untying the bridle, he climbed on the fence railing and straddled the mare. He hated to ride her without a saddle, but it was a short distance, and she was obviously not concerned. "Okay, let's go."

No sooner had he said the words than Lady broke into a gallop. Squeezing his knees, he got her to slow before coming up on Riley.

She looked up as he and Lady came abreast of her. "You can let her run. When you get there, put her in the north corral.

I have to prepare a stall for her. Cole forgot to let me know she was coming."

Her tone brooked no argument. Whether it was her attitude or her criticism of Cole, he wasn't sure, but irritation ran up his spine. He was all for being polite; however, he didn't take this job to be ordered about as if he were a greenhorn. Without a word, he let Lady have her head.

By the time he slowed her down, he was ready to leave. His job was to pick up the horses and drop them off, complete with story and paperwork.

Paperwork. He'd left that in the truck. He'd grab it once he moved Lady into the corral. Both corrals were empty, which meant the horses must still be in the barn. He jumped down from Lady's back and opened the gate. Taking the bridle off, he let her inside and closed her in. As she pranced around in a circle taking her victory lap, he headed for the barn, intending to hang up the bridle then return to his truck.

"Hey, boy." He nodded to a black quarter horse who eyed him from an open stall with a roof attached to the barn. As he took his first step inside, a nicker from within had him stopping, Riley's story about Angel reminding him this wasn't a typical stable. This was a horse rescue ranch, which meant he had no idea what phobias or issues the horses stabled there might have.

Looking over his shoulder, he found the black watching him. He'd bet money that horse was housed outside for a reason. Retreating from the barn, he strode to the north corral and laid the bridle over the fence.

He could hear Riley talking to Cyclone as the big horse pulled the stack of lumber. Quickly, he strode to the truck and opened the passenger door. Heat from sitting in the sun washed over him from inside. He'd forgotten to leave the windows down when he saw Riley climbing the fence to jump on Cyclone.

Bad move in the Sonoran Desert in the middle of summer. Grabbing the folder, he left the door open and met Riley as she and the horse pulled into the parking area from around the side of the house.

She brought Cyclone to a halt. "Sorry about that." She gestured with her head toward the dirt road she'd just walked up. "I'm not used to having anyone around here, except Annette, and she doesn't come out in the heat anymore. I appreciate you helping with the big guy." She patted the horse, who had to be at least sixteen hands high.

In the face of her apology, his irritation lessened. "You're welcome." He held out the folder. "Here's the paperwork."

She crinkled her nose, making her appear very young. "Hold that thought, will you? I just want to get Cy unhooked and fed. I'll have to do another haul with him today, but I think he'll behave for at least an hour."

He didn't actually have anywhere he needed to be, so he nodded.

Next time he saw Cole, he would definitely ask him about his ranch hand. Did he know she criticized him? Cole had a lot on his plate being Captain in the Canterbury Fire Department and running a horse rescue. He certainly didn't need an employee griping about him.

Then again, she had a point. She did seem to be the lone worker. Not comfortable with getting in the middle of something he knew nothing about, he wandered toward the barn and leaned against it as Riley efficiently unhooked Cyclone and walked past him, bringing the horse into his stall and feeding him.

When she was done, she brushed her hands on her jeans and approached. "Is there anymore to the story of Lady other than she's a little older and obviously competitive?"

He glanced over his shoulder. Lady had stopped her

victory lap and stood watching them. More than likely, she was waiting for Cyclone to emerge again. He faced Riley. "The competitiveness was not in the paperwork. Just that she and two geldings were being transferred to Last Chance. All three are older and are meant to live out the rest of their lives here."

She held out her hand for the folder. "Here? That's going to be costly. I've seen horses like Lady live to thirty-two."

So had he, when they were well cared for, and if they had good genes. "I don't think that will be a problem. The old man left a trust for the horses."

Her eyes rounded. "A trust? For horses?" Her eyes lit with understanding. "So that's why the grandson wants to be sure they're well cared for. He wants to make sure Cole isn't taking the money and not treating them right. He obviously doesn't know Cole. He's as protective of his horses as I am."

Now he was confused. First, she sounded like a disgruntled employee and now she sounded completely loyal. "I'm sure that's part of it, but like I said, I think there's some grief associated with the whole scenario."

She shrugged. "Whatever. If it's going to happen, it's going to happen."

He had no idea if she meant people passing on or if she meant the grandson coming, but he wasn't completely comfortable with either thought. Better to leave and let her do her job. He'd done his. "Everything there is to know is in there." He nodded to the open folder in her hands. "I'll be back in a couple days with the other two."

Her head snapped up, a frown on her face. "A couple days? Why the delay?"

He shrugged, anxious to be going now. "I'm not sure. Again, I think the grandchildren may be reminiscing."

She looked past him at Lady. "I hope she doesn't mind

being without them. The last thing I need is a horse who won't eat."

"Why wouldn't she eat?"

She took a deep breath as if she needed to be patient with him. "Before I came, they had three almost starved horses arrive here. One wouldn't eat unless she was in the same enclosure with the other two. They almost lost her before they discovered the problem."

"How'd they figure it out? Was it just dumb luck?"

"Whisper."

He glanced toward the barn and lowered his voice. "Was it just luck?"

Her brow crinkled before a half-smile lifted her lips. "No, I meant Whisper figured it out. She's, well, an animal whisperer for lack of a better term."

His doubt must have shown on his face because she shook her head. "I know, but if you'd seen some of the things that woman has learned and done with animals, you'd be a believer."

He doubted that, but then again, he was probably the only non-superstitious firefighter for a hundred miles.

She closed the folder and stuck it under her arm as she hooked her right thumb in her front pocket. "We receive all the problem horses. The bruised, the battered, the starved, the neglected, the unwanted. Just like with people, that takes a toll on them. My goal is to make them whole again. The more I know, the better the chances of making that happen."

He had to admit, not only did she pique his curiosity about the horses, but also about her. She was as hard to pin down as a wildfire. "Do you have a lot in here now?" He found himself gesturing toward the barn opening.

"We have a few." She turned and headed inside. "Some of these will be going home eventually." She looked over her shoulder. "Cole's relatives get attached. The big guy is actually Dr. Jenna's, our vet, but she doesn't have a working ranch, so he stays with us. He came from a rescue place in Dallas. Don't know if you noticed, but he has some burn scars on his back from being in a fire."

He had noticed them. Burn scars were his specialty.

She stopped between two stalls of brown and white paints, one obviously still a yearling. "This is Lucky and his mom, Macey. Macey was brought here because her owner thought she looked more like a cow than a horse because of her markings. Lucky was born here and is Charlotte's. That's Logan's daughter. The one outside is Logan's. That's Black Jack. He's claustrophobic thanks to being inside a mine when it partly caved in, so Logan is planning to build a shelter for him over at Dr. Jenna's before moving all of them over there."

"Logan?" It sounded as if he was supposed to know who that was.

"Cole's cousin." She moved to another stall where a brown colt was suckling on a beautiful black Frisian. "This is Nizohoni and her colt, Phoenix. These are the two I saved." Without elaborating she moved to another stall where a black and white paint greeted her. "This is my baby. I saved her too by buying her off my former employer. I don't know who trained her, but she's the smartest horse I've ever met, and I've met a lot."

As the rough-edged Riley hugged the stately horse, he suddenly sensed that she only showed that kind of affection to her mount. Now why would he think that? "You saved them?"

She shrugged as she moved on to the other side of the barn. "That's the whole point of this place. This little one is Tiny Dancer. For some unknown reason, even to Whisper, Cyclone is infatuated with this little thing."

At that information, he took a second look at the small

paint with almost bowed legs. She was as dainty and small as Cyclone was big. It reminded him of his first best friend in high school. She was very short and feminine. Made him want to take care of her even though they were never an item. "Maybe he just wants to protect her."

She met his gaze for the first time since entering the barn. "I'll suggest that to Whisper." She moved to the next stall, which stood empty. "I'll put Lady in here and the two geldings in the next two stalls, unless they need to see each other."

See each other? When Cole told him he ran a horse rescue, he hadn't truly understood what that might entail. "I don't think that's necessary, but if there're any peculiarities, I'm sure Wyatt will let you know."

She continued to the tack area. "By Wyatt, I assume you mean the grandson." She grimaced even as she dropped the folder on a shelf and grabbed a pair of gloves.

He chuckled. "He's not that bad. Like I said, it's just his way of keeping his grandfather a little longer." He expected some show of sympathy. Most women would express empathy for a person who lost someone close to them, but not Riley.

"I need to get Lady's stall ready then move some of these horses out to the north corral before heading back to Cole's with Cyclone. By then I should be able to work on that fence rail. Is there anything else I need to know?"

Once again, her tone turned authoritative. He stiffened, more used to giving the orders than taking them. "No, that's it. I'll be back in a couple days."

"This time I'll be ready." She turned toward him and offered her hand. "Good to meet you, Garrett. Welcome to Last Chance."

Surprised, he shook her hand before she pulled on the gloves and headed for the loft, where bags of shavings were stacked. Clearly dismissed, he strode out of the barn and toward his truck.

He'd always been one of those people who could meet someone and within minutes sense what they were about. That wasn't the case with Riley. She bothered him like a flame that won't go out. He wasn't used to being unsure about a person.

He couldn't help but watch her lead Cyclone back out to the south corral. As she closed the gate behind the "big guy," she caught sight of him and gave him a lazy salute kind of wave before striding back to the barn, her mind on nothing but her work.

On one hand, he liked her. She appeared to have a good heart when it came to animals. For people, not so much. She was obviously a good worker, but seemed to hold a grudge for some reason. One minute she was almost warm and the next telling him what to do.

He closed the passenger door of the truck before walking around to the driver's side. Reaching in from where he stood, he put the keys in the ignition and turned it on, putting the air conditioner on full blast before closing the door and striding to the front of the pick-up.

Riley had returned Cyclone to the south corral with the broken fence. Obviously, she wasn't concerned that he'd leave.

Lady was prancing in small circles near her end of the north corral as Cyclone stood watching her. And to think, some people believed animals had no emotions. If he were to hazard a guess on what was taking place, he'd say that Lady was being a sore winner and Cyclone was stewing over it. Then again, he wasn't a horse whisperer.

He had, however, considered himself a bit of a people whisperer though, but with Riley, he doubted anyone knew what made her tick. Shaking his head, he returned to the driver's side of the truck and climbed into the now cooler cab.

Putting the truck into gear, he scanned the immediate vicinity for one more glance of her, but she was still busy in the barn. He hadn't known what to expect when he accepted Cole's job offer, but now he was looking forward to returning to Last Chance, even if it was just to study Riley O'Hare further.

And studying was all it would be. He knew better than to have an interest in a woman. That door closed five years ago.

Riley finished the last bite of mashed potatoes and wiped her mouth. Though she preferred having dinner with just Annette and Ed, she had to admit, Cole's grandmother went all out when the whole family came by...or most of it.

Cole, the big sometimes cowboy and all-the-time firefighter, had offered her room and board to "help out" on Last Chance. However, her room and board were actually provided by his grandmother in the main house. Her "boss" lived in his new home with his wife, Lacey, a petite blonde who had him wrapped around her little finger.

She liked the arrangements because, except for Annette babysitting Logan's daughter three days a week, it was normally pretty quiet. In addition, despite Annette's age, she was a tough rancher through and through, the kind of woman Riley liked.

"Are you all packed and ready for your cruise?" Lacey flicked her braid over her shoulder and looked at Annette expectantly.

The older woman shrugged. "As much as I'm willing to lug on a plane and a boat." She glanced at her husband, who was grinning ear to ear. "This one will need a separate truck for his luggage."

Ed laughed loudly as he put his arm around his wife. "It's not every day my better half turns seventy-five."

Dr. Jenna, who was five-feet-five inches of no nonsense, looked at Logan. "Now that's true love."

The man nodded before turning to his daughter in a high chair between him and Annette. "What do you think, Charlotte? Is that true love?"

Three-year-old Charlotte dropped her sippy cup at that moment and leaned over her chair, her hand opening and closing. "I want cup."

"I want my cup, please." Annette bent over and put it back on the tray for the little girl, eliciting a grin before she promptly lifted it with two hands and drank. The older woman's brow furrowed as she studied her grandson. "Are you sure you can handle her for two weeks?"

Logan brushed his daughter's hair back out of her eyes. "I'm looking forward to spending time with my daughter."

Dr. Jenna chimed in. "And we're going up to the Grand Canyon for the weekend."

Trace, Logan's brother and the easy-going one in the family with a ready smile, shook his head. "You know she's not going to remember seeing it. She's too young."

"Who said anything about seeing the Grand Canyon?" Logan smirked. "We're just going up there to get out of this blistering heat."

Whisper leaned in toward Riley. "I don't see anything wrong with the heat." Then she returned her attention to the family. "We're headed to Vegas. Uncle Joey has had that city on his bucket list since before his stroke, so Trace and I are making it happen."

Riley couldn't keep silent any longer. "What about you, Cole? Are you off for the weekend, too?"

He shook his head. "No, I'm planning to start work on the deck I promised Lacey."

She stifled a grin. Wait until he discovered the lumber gone.

Annette passed the plate with two T-bone steaks still on it. "Here, Riley, you need to have more. You deserve it after having to repair that fence rail and get the barn ready for the new horse on such short notice."

The older woman gave her a conspiratorial wink, which definitely made her feel appreciated.

"Thank you." Without hesitation, she took a steak off the tray.

A groan sounded from across the table. "I'm sorry, Riley. I forgot to tell you. I went into the station at two this morning and spaced it."

Cole's apology took the edge off her irritation. "It wasn't anything I couldn't handle. Though I was surprised to see a new driver."

"You got a new driver?" Lacey turned on her husband. "What happened to Manuel? I liked him."

Cole looked away and sighed. Riley almost felt bad for him. "Looks like I need to apologize again. Manuel moved to New Mexico to live on his daughter's ranch. She's expecting their first grandchild."

"Oh, well, that's a good reason." Lacey's smile returned. "Who did you hire on such short notice?"

"An old classmate of mine, Garrett Walker."

Trace frowned. "If he's your age, does he realize the pay won't keep a roof over his head?"

Cole nodded. "Yes. It's not his only income."

Riley swallowed the piece of steak she'd been chewing. "I don't think he realized exactly how different our horses are." She smirked. "After seeing Cyclone break the fence rail, he thought I was next."

Whisper grunted. "That horse wouldn't hurt a rabbit."

The phrase was *wouldn't hurt a fly*, but she wasn't about to correct Whisper. "He said he's bringing the other two horses in a couple days and that the grandson of the deceased is also going to arrive?"

This time it was Annette who jumped on Cole. "You didn't tell me we'd be having company while we're gone. I need to make up the other bedroom upstairs, get out towels, prep more food. I only made enough for Riley for the week."

Her boss's face froze, his lack of communication seriously catching up to him. Before he could apologize once again, his wife saved him. "Don't worry, Annette. Cole and I will be here. If I need to help Riley cook up some extra food, I don't mind, or I can have the young man over to our house."

Riley just couldn't let Lacey's comment go. "Or he can cook his own food." She was proud of herself for not voicing her real thought which was that the boy could cook his own *damn* food. She'd planned to cook for herself. That Annette had prepared meals for her didn't sit well. It wasn't like she was family, nor did she want to be. Being alone and separate was better.

Whisper laughed. "What she said. Annette, you enjoy your trip. We're all adults here. We can take care of the place while you're gone." Whisper rose. "Now if I'm not mistaken, there's a new horse in the barn that I need to meet. Dr. Jenna, want to grab your bag?"

Logan's fiancée wiped her mouth and pushed back her chair. "Yes, I will."

Whisper grabbed Riley's shoulder. "What's the new horse's name?"

She put her forkful of meat back down on the plate. "It's Lady. From what I understand, she's just old, but I noticed a bit of competitiveness in her this afternoon. You want me to introduce you?"

Whisper's hand on her shoulder tightened. "No. We're good."

She filled her mouth with meat to show she'd stay, but she'd be done shortly and planned to join them. As the conversation moved to other topics, she focused on wolfing down her food.

By time she'd finished, Lacey had offered to take care of setting up the bedroom across the hall from her. She didn't mind sharing a bathroom with men, but a teenage boy who thought he knew more about horses than her was bound to be a problem.

She rose and brought her plate to the counter.

Cole stepped up next to her to add his to the sink. "Hey, I'm sorry about all that. I've got too much on my plate."

"I know." The question was, what was he going to do about it? "It happens." She shrugged. She wanted things to change, but she wasn't willing to make a commitment. The rescue horses deserved someone who would stay with them. Staying wasn't her forte.

She'd been at Last Chance a year and eight months now. That was edging up toward being forever for her. So why wasn't she leaving?

"I can't let it happen." Cole's voice was filled with self-recrimination. "These horses depend on me. I need to get my act together."

Ah, now *that* she understood. How many times had she said that to herself? She smirked as she headed for the doorway. "Good luck with that." Not hanging around to hear his reply, she strode down the hall and out onto the front porch.

The sun, though starting its descent, was still strong with no clouds to steal its summer rays.

It was still better than Afghanistan. She let her gaze roam past the barn to the desert beyond, scanning for movement. It was a habit born out of survival. The Arizona desert was far different and far safer than the one overseas, but she couldn't help it. She doubted she'd ever stop watching.

Or checking. Her hands automatically went to her pockets, taking inventory by feel, another habit she'd developed while deployed. One lip balm, packet of ibuprofen, and mints in the front pockets, SOG pocket knife and bandana in the back pockets.

Satisfied all was where it should be and the horizon was safe, she jogged down the steps. She had come a long way in the last few years. No more nightmares of being buried alive. No more binge eating or talking to herself. She was almost normal. Maybe in a few more years, she'd stop checking her supplies, too.

Stepping into the slightly cooler shade of the barn, she heard the two other women in the stall on the right. She felt more comfortable around them than around Lacey. Leaning on the door, she found Dr. Jenna examining the mare, Whisper standing out of the way.

"Did you learn anything?"

Whisper kept her gaze on Lady. "She doesn't think she's old. But you were right, she's definitely competitive." The woman shrugged. "It feels like she'd had a good life so far."

"Does she miss her companions?" She hoped it was bothering her more than it did the horse that the two geldings wouldn't arrive for another couple days.

Whisper's mouth quirked up. "Actually, she likes having time away from them. I get the feeling they bother her sometimes."

At that news, she relaxed. "Good to know. I'll be sure to give her some girl time then even after they arrive."

"Good idea."

Dr. Jenna returned her ophthalmoscope to her black bag. "She's a very healthy mare for her age. I just need to check her medical record, but unless she's behind on any shots, she's as healthy as Cyclone."

"Only with less issues." Riley couldn't help adding. After all, the big guy was Dr. Jenna's.

Jenna shrugged. "If Cyclone didn't have issues, I wouldn't have fallen in love with him." She picked up her heavy bag. "That's what Last Chance is for, horses with issues."

Riley opened the stall door so the two women could exit. Maybe that's why she was here so long. Last Chance seemed to be the perfect place for a person like herself…a person with issues.

Chapter Three

Garrett sat at the bar of the Black Mustang and nursed his beer. Tomorrow, he'd drive out to Cave Creek to pick up the other two horses from Wyatt, who would probably follow him back to Last Chance and make sure Riley gave them everything they needed.

He didn't envy her that. Just from what he'd seen, Wyatt was overly picky. The only reason he'd been patient with the man is the pain of loss in his eyes. It was one of the reasons he was sitting at the Black Mustang, hoping to catch Cole when he came in before he and his men took over the pool table in the back. Cole, who was very by-the-book himself, might have a difficult time with Wyatt.

But that wasn't the main reason he waited. He'd become even more curious about Riley O'Hare, especially when she'd invaded his dreams last night. Calling what he had a dream was being generous. It was like an old-fashioned acid trip. It included Riley riding a winged Cyclone, encouraging him to pull Cole's new house up into the sky. While he'd been herding wild mustangs directly into the barn, which had grown to five stories high inside and looked more like a parking garage. He'd jerked awake just as Cole's house landed on the open top story of the barn.

At least there'd been no fire. No trees either. That fact alone had him feeling like a normal human being. He'd had "normal" dreams for almost a year now, though none quite as odd as last night's.

A hand landed on his shoulder. "Hey, Walker! Isn't this a little late for you to be out? What happen? You take a nap today?"

He knew that voice without even looking. "Mason." Turning around, he pushed the firefighter away. "What are you doing here? Mommy lift your curfew?"

Scott Mason, who was the size of a pro linebacker, laughed. "I thought you'd moved up north."

"I did, but I'm back."

"Man, you look good. From what I'd heard, you were at death's door."

Obviously, Cole hadn't said anything. He shrugged. "Exaggeration and hearsay."

Mason, who sported a bald head and a mustache now, moved a stool out of his way and stood against the bar. "Hey, Cutter. Two drafts. One for my friend here."

The bartender with the earing nodded as he moved for the cold glasses.

"So, where you living now?"

Garrett swallowed the rest of his current beer before answering. "In Wickenburg."

"Ack, Canterbury is better. If you want to move, just say the word. I can get you out of your lease in a heartbeat."

"No lease. Got my own place. You don't think I'd dare entrust my living quarters to you girls, do you?"

Mason laughed again, his bigger than life smile and personality a hit with the ladies. The man was only serious when he was on the job and even then, it was sporadic. "You should join us for a few games." With his head, he gestured toward the pool table at the back of the bar. "I wouldn't mind drinking for free all night."

Garrett pointedly looked behind Mason. "We? You still playing with imaginary friends?"

"Yeah, you know Hatcher and Clark. We also recruited Alvarez and Maddox after Jenkins and Garcia transferred to the Peoria station. They all *imagine* themselves good pool players." Another laugh followed that statement. "You should join us. We need some—ah shit, they're here."

He turned in his chair to see all four Canterbury firefighters walking in.

"Look who I found!" Mason yelled loud enough to be heard in the parking lot.

They all came over to greet him, Cole last. Beers were ordered as he traded insults with each of them. They hadn't changed as far as he could see, except maybe brawnier. Cole must have prevailed on the chief to add the gym he'd always wanted when he first transferred.

They probably wouldn't see changes in him either. But a lot had happened in the five years he'd been gone.

Cole, as usual, took charge. "Why don't you boys start? I'll be over for the next round. I'm going to see if I can't get Walker to join us."

As the firefighters headed for the pool table, Cole took the seat next to him. "I'm guessing you being here tonight wasn't a coincidence."

He lifted his draft in salute. "I always said you were the smart one."

Cole's gaze moved from his. "Smart, maybe, but lately I've been dropping balls everywhere. I can't even remember where some of them rolled to."

"Too much on your plate?"

He nodded.

"I hate to add more to it, but I wanted to talk to you about Wyatt."

"Wyatt?" Cole's brows lowered in confusion.

The man really did have too much on his plate. "Yes, Wyatt Ford, the grandson of Earl Ford where the most recent rescue horses are coming from?"

"Yes. Like I said, can't even find where the stupid balls have rolled." Cole took a swig of beer then set his glass on the bar. "What about Wyatt? When I talked to him at the ranch, he was pretty broken up. Had a hard time staying focused. He kept repeating that he had to be sure the horses were well cared for. That's why I invited him to stay at Last Chance for a while until he was satisfied they would have a good life there."

"Yeah, I got the feeling his obsession about the horses had to do with his loss as well, but it can be irritating."

"How so?"

He didn't want to make Wyatt appear a pain in the ass, but he very easily could be. "When I picked up the mare, he had me read two pages of instructions on how to transport the horses."

Cole picked up his beer and took another swallow before responding. "That could be a problem, especially if he shows up at Last Chance with an entire book. Those horses are just older. They're not nearly as complicated as others we've had. His loss of perspective could rub people the wrong way."

That's what he was afraid would happen. "Do you think it's the loss of his grandfather or just the way he is?"

"I have no idea. I was there the day after the old man passed and Wyatt was a mess. I barely spent fifteen minutes with him. I guess we'll find out."

Except it wouldn't be Cole and himself who would have

to deal with the man, which brought him to his real reason for catching Cole. "Or rather, Riley will find out."

This time Cole let out a heavy sigh. "Yeah, that. If Wyatt's like you say, that's going to rub Riley all the wrong way. Damn."

"What's her story?" He tried to make it a nonchalant comment, but from the odd look Cole gave him, he didn't quite pull it off.

"I don't know much about her. She was the stable manager for one of the land developers in Phoenix. He was losing money hand over fist, selling off his horses to make up for it. Then his planned community didn't get approved by the city and he went berserk, taking it out on a new colt. She called animal welfare on him."

"She called out her boss? That's biting the hand that feeds you."

"I don't think she cares who feeds her as long as the horses are treated right, which made her perfect for Last Chance. I had a lot of help there for a while. Logan and Trace had both moved into my grandparents' place, but they've since moved out again. Then Dillon stayed for a while."

"Your little brother?" Last he'd seen of Dillon, he was dancing to the tune of his mother's fiddle.

Cole nodded. "Yeah, he'd finally had it with my mother, but he missed breeding his horses, so as soon as he had something to hold over her head, he went home. Now Riley is the only dependable ranch hand I have. You wouldn't want more work, would you?"

Work with Riley O'Hare? He had to wonder how that would go over. "Do you think Riley would be open to another hand? She seems…" He wasn't sure how to word it without making her sound cantankerous.

"Short? Demanding? Impatient? Straight as an arrow?"

He chuckled. Cole obviously knew Riley well enough. "All of the above."

"She doesn't make it a secret that she needs help, so she can't exactly be picky. Besides, you know horses, so you two would get along well. Why? Did she piss you off?"

"No, just got irritated a couple times. She has a way about her."

Cole took another swallow of beer. "You mean when she gives orders. That's her military background. She's a veteran."

That had never occurred to him, but now that he had that piece of information, a lot of the other pieces of her personality fell into place. "Did she see action?"

"Yeah, but she hasn't spoken about it. You know how it is. You can't make someone talk about stuff like that if they don't want to, right?" Cole's gaze held more understanding than he was comfortable with.

He lifted his beer. "Right."

Cole clinked his glass in agreement. "She wasn't with the land developer very long. I think she moves around a lot."

"When I asked her how long she'd worked at Last Chance, she said for her it was a long time."

Cole gave another heartfelt sigh. "If she leaves, I'm screwed. Trace and Logan still help out, but with three more horses and who knows how many more we'll be receiving this year, I can't afford to lose her. I pulled Trace from picking up horses to taking the calls on cases. Logan has his daughter with him four days a week, so I need him for the bigger projects on the three other days. It would certainly help me sleep better at night if you'd think about taking on more."

He wouldn't admit it, but knowing Riley was there made him hesitate. With both of them being used to command, it might not work. "I'm still settling in. Let me think about it."

"That's all I can ask."

"Hey, Cole! You ready to get your ass kicked?" Mason's voice had everyone in the bar turning toward him.

Cole held his arm up then stood. "Cutter, give me four more drafts." He dropped cash on the bar.

"Not running a tab?" Garrett wouldn't be surprised if Cole didn't drink another beer all night. He wasn't the type to drink and drive.

"Don't need to. I plan to win any drinks I need off of Mason." He leaned down as if anyone could hear him. "He's still a pissant lightweight. Three beers and I'm home free."

Garrett grinned. Some things never changed.

Cole clapped a hand on his shoulder. "Think about my offer?"

"I will."

Cole scooped up two drafts in each large hand and headed for the back.

He was glad Cole hadn't invited him to play. He wasn't up for the camaraderie just yet. Being around others meant having to answer questions, especially with men he knew. He planned to ease back into life in Canterbury and Wickenburg one day at a time.

One person at a time.

Riley closed the gate on the newly repaired south corral. Phoenix was running circles around his mom, his little head going up and down. So far, he seemed to only have external scars from the whipping he'd taken from her last employer.

Lucky watched from where he stood next to Macey. The two colts were starting to enjoy each other's company, but Lucky was always hesitant to make the first move of the day. In another half hour, Macey and Nizhoni would be standing in the shade with Tiny Dancer, and the two young ones would be playing despite the heat. Black Jack liked to think of himself as the leader of their little band and usually stayed with the mares. She understood his need to be with others. She may not be a social animal herself, but being alone was dangerous.

In the north corral, Lady stood watching. She'd done fine with Cyclone on their walk a couple days ago, but Riley wasn't going to risk her with the other mares and young ones quite yet. She'd have Garrett put Lady's companions in with her when they arrived. As far as she was concerned, Cyclone needed a day to chill, but she hadn't ridden Domino in a couple days.

She pushed away from the fence and started for her horse. Domino was a sweetheart. Unlike her owner, she got along with everyone. That's probably the only reason the two of them worked so well together.

"Hey, girl. You up for a ride today?"

The black and white paint set its head over the stall door.

"I thought so. Let me get your gear." Striding over to the tack room, she pulled down Domino's bridle and saddle. Dumping them in the middle of the barn, she had to admit, the price she'd paid for her horse was far less than she was worth, despite the scumbag's attempt to squeeze out every penny. Domino was priceless.

Heat prickled across her skin at the thought. Having something she valued wasn't smart, but even the thought of moving on without Domino had her hands fisting.

She shook off her uncomfortable feelings and opened the stall door. Clicking her tongue, she waited as Domino walked out to stop at the pile on the floor. "Have I told you what a bright spot in my day you are?"

The horse's ears shifted to listen to her.

She set about prepping Domino for the saddle. She'd never had a horse stand so still while being saddled before. Everything about Domino made her easy to love. "I wish I knew who your trainer was. Too bad your good behavior couldn't wear off on a couple of the horses around here." She sent Cyclone a dirty look, but he wasn't paying attention to her. He was staring at the open barn doors.

At the sound of a truck, she finished cinching the saddle then grabbed up the bridle. "Come on, Domino. Let's see who's here." She patted the horse on her neck and the two of them walked out into the hot Arizona sun together.

She'd expected to see Garrett with the horse trailer, but instead it was Cole and Lacey on their way off the ranch. He put the truck into park and hopped out, leaving the driver side door open.

"Where you headed? I thought you were working on the deck today." She waved back the way he'd come.

His jaw tightened. "Apparently, I forgot I'd told my mother we would see her for my parents' anniversary celebration. It's their thirty sixth."

Oh, that wasn't good. Who celebrated their thirty-sixth? She looked past him and waved to Lacey. The woman shook her head, obviously not happy. That Lacey and Cole's mom didn't get along was a well-known fact.

If she were to choose a side, it would be Lacey's after what Cole's mother had pulled, but she no longer had to worry about family dynamics. "You just going down for the day or overnight?"

Cole ground his teeth before answering. "It's supposed to be all weekend."

At his tone, it sounded as if he'd try to find a way to leave a lot earlier. She didn't blame him. Again, not her problem. "Okay."

He moved his gaze to her horse. "I don't like leaving you here alone, especially with more horses coming and…"

When he didn't finish, she grew impatient. "And?"

"It may be a bit uncomfortable having Wyatt here, but do me a favor and cut him some slack. He just lost his grandfather, who he was very close to, as in practically raised him."

Ah, so Cole was afraid she'd bite the kid's head off the second he tried to tell her what to do. He was right. "Tell you what. The first time the boy pisses me off, I'll call you. Then you can honestly tell your mom you have an emergency at the ranch."

Instead of being relieved, he appeared startled. "He's not a boy. He's nearing thirty."

Really? And he was that attached to his grandfather's horses? She hated to tell Cole, but it could get ugly fast. "I'll still call you."

He didn't look reassured, but then again, she wasn't going to make it easy on him. The sooner he realized he needed to delegate, the sooner life at the ranch would run smoothly.

Finally, he sighed. "I would appreciate that. I know you know what you're doing. I wouldn't have hired you on if I didn't. Do the best you can with him. That's all I can ask."

"Look at it this way. If he has the horses' best interests at heart, we'll get along just fine." She chuckled at the doubt in Cole's green eyes and slapped him on the arm. "Go do your duty. It's the right thing to do. I'm sure I'll manage just fine. It's not like I haven't before."

"I know. I'm working on getting more help."

The horn blared from the truck. "Come on, Cole. The sooner we do this, the sooner we can get back!" The sweet smile Lacey threw her husband was full of shit.

He glanced over his shoulder at his wife before facing her again.

"Go." She nodded toward the truck. "I can handle this."

"Right. Thanks. Remind me to give you a raise."

She raised her brow. "I will."

With a quick nod, he strode back to Lacey. As he drove the truck down the long dirt drive, she shook her head. Only Cole would drive slow enough to avoid kicking up dust. Then again, with the destination he was headed for, she wasn't all that surprised he dragged his heels.

Turning back to Domino, she gave the horse a hug. "Thank you for being so dependable, sweet thing."

Her horse leaned her head against her, perfectly happy with her, flaws and all. Hell, compared to herself, Domino was damn perfect. "Okay, enough of the gushy stuff, let's ride." Fitting the bridle on Domino, she gave her one more pat then mounted.

Once more she scanned the area before kicking her mount into a gallop down the dirt drive to Cole and Lacey's house. She reined her in as they reached the path Whisper had worn across the desert with her regular trips on Spirit from her trailer to the main house. Tempted to follow it and give Domino some good exercise, she glanced back over her shoulder.

A dust cloud from an approaching truck, told her that would have to wait. Turning Domino around, she gave her her head, the horse slowing automatically as she approached the parking area in front of the main house again.

"What the hell?" Recognizing Whisper's blue truck, she dismounted.

Trace drove, Uncle Joey in the middle of the front bench seat and Whisper on the passenger side. The truck came to a stop and Whisper jumped out. "Hey, I need you to look after this for me."

Riley strode forward as Whisper headed for the back of the pick-up. "I thought you were on your way to Vegas?"

Whisper opened the tail gate. "We are, but this guy was on the side of the highway." A small dog licked Whisper's face. "Don't worry, Riley's gonna take care of you until I get back. I know it's hard to believe, but you'll be safe with me."

Riley stared at the four-legged animal. "What are you talking about?"

Whisper stepped back from the truck. "Come on. Time to get down."

The dog paced across the tailgate and whined.

"Come here."

The dog sat on its haunches, refusing to leave the truck.

"Riley, come here."

"Oh, I thought you were talking to the dog." The woman's tone of voice certainly made it sound that way.

Whisper rolled her eyes as if that was the stupidest assumption. "He won't come down because he thinks I'm abandoning him. That's what his last owners did."

She knew that feeling, so she walked over. "Now what?"

"Now, go over to him. Let him sniff your hand."

She'd been around dogs. They slobbered all over a person. "I'll only do this for you." She gave Whisper a serious look. Walking up to the tailgate, she let the dog sniff her hand. Its tail started to wag just as it licked her. "Ugh." She pulled her hand back.

"Give me a break. You get more germs feeding your horse. Think of him like a little horse."

Little was the operative word in that statement. The dog couldn't be more than twelve pounds. He, if it was a he, was mostly white with some brown spots scattered over his body. Not really spots so much as blobs of light brown to match the desert.

"I need you to take care of him until we get back."

"Me?" She snapped her head around to give Whisper a scowl. "Why me?"

Whisper gestured down the road toward Cole's home. "Because he's too busy and she's not an animal person. You are."

Crap. Everyone was gone. Even Dr. Jenna. "Can't you bring him to Dr. Jenna's office. Doesn't she do boarding?"

Whisper took the two steps that brought them nose to nose. "Did you not hear what I just said?" She pointed to the dog. "He was abandoned. You want me to stick him in a room full of other dogs who have been abandoned for the weekend?"

Riley had never backed down from a fight, not even when the dude was twice as big as her, but staring into Whisper's steel gray eyes, her instinct told her she needed to treat the woman like a commanding officer. "I see your point."

"Good." Whisper turned to the dog and laid a hand on its neck. "I'll be back in a few days and then we'll go home."

The dog looked at her as if it understood.

"You're going to stay with Riley here until I get back." Without warning, she scooped the dog off the tailgate and set him on the ground. Immediately, his nose caught a scent and he followed it to a pile of dog poop left behind by Butterball, Dr. Jenna's English bulldog.

Riley grimaced before turning her attention back to Whisper. "What's his name?"

Whisper slammed the tailgate closed. "I don't know yet. That will take more time than I have right now. He looks like a Jack Russel Terrier, but I doubt he's pure, which is a good thing." She brushed her hands together and headed for the passenger door. "We have to get going if we're going to make the first night's show. Uncle Joey has his heart set on it."

Great. On top of caring for all the horses and dealing with

Wyatt, now she had a mutt to babysit. If Cole didn't get his act together soon, she was outta there.

"Hey, watch him." Whisper stood on the running board of the truck and pointed to the dog who just wandered into the barn. "Don't let him out of your sight. He's domestic. Doubt he had more than a fenced in yard before. This open space is bound to be overwhelming."

Overwhelming? For a dog? She nodded as if she understood just to get them out of her hair. Then she strode for the barn. The dog better not disturb the horses or it was going into its own stall and staying there all weekend.

He was abandoned. Or maybe she'd just keep him in there while she was in the barn. Only if he didn't behave.

Trace honked the horn behind her, and she stopped to wave them on. Satisfied they were on their way, she stepped around the corner into the shade of the barn. A scuffle inside had her scanning the area, but there was no dog.

"Well, shit. Where are you Dog?"

She headed for the open stall at the back when Dog came out, a rat in its mouth. She stopped. "I guess you're good for something."

Dog trotted over and sat directly in front of her. His right paw lifted, and he pawed her jeans.

"Yes, I see you got a rat. That's good." His big brown eyes were wide as he looked at her, one eyebrow lifting slightly higher than the other. "What? I said that was good." For Pete's sake. "Good boy."

Dog wagged his tail, apparently happy with that before standing and trotting outside.

"I hope you're going to bury it, too." She followed Dog and kept an eye on him as she walked to Domino. So much for a good long run. She patted the horse on her back. "I wonder if the little guy could keep up."

Dog stopped beneath the large mesquite tree on the other side of the dirt road that led to Cole's and dropped the rat. Annette wouldn't be excited to find the dead animal so close to her front porch.

Riley started for the tree, but halted as the dog began to dig. This looked promising. Turning back to Domino, she grasped the reins and walked her toward the shady side of the house, all the while watching Dog. She didn't want to lose him. As much as she admired Whisper, she was also cautious. The woman was unpredictable, often carrying a Glock, she called Sal, in the waistband of her jeans. Anyone who named their gun had a special relationship with it.

When Dog finished his hole, instead of dropping the rat in it as she'd hoped, he lay down in the dark earth.

"Really?" She shook her head. Whisper may think Riley was good with animals, but that wasn't true at all. As a child, she'd forgotten to feed at least three gold fish, lost two gerbils in the house, and the racoon she'd been trying to feed outside bit her. She held up her wrist to inspect the back for the old scar. Her mom had been more upset than she had. She'd taken after her Senior Master Sergeant Air Force father. The man with no emotions at all, or at least that was how it seemed next to her mother.

"What are we supposed to do with him, Domino?" She absently stroked the black section of her horse's withers. She wasn't surprised when she received no response. Domino was used to her chatting with her. It was a lot easier than talking to the shrink the Army had made her see when she'd returned.

Glancing toward the road, she scanned for the telltale dust of an approaching truck, but all was still. It was already mid-morning and still Lady's cohorts had not arrived. She hated standing around doing nothing. Looking over to Dog she found him staring at her, his tongue hanging out his mouth, his head slightly cocked.

Were dogs supposed to do that? She didn't remember seeing one with its tongue hanging out. Crap, she hoped he wasn't sick or something. He looked like he was dying of thirst. "Hey Dog, you want some water?"

The animal's ears perked up, but he didn't move.

If he was thirsty, he wasn't very smart. Not knowing what else to do, she tied Domino to the porch railing, not that the horse would go anywhere, then walked up the steps. "I'll get you some water. I doubt Annette will want you in the house anyway. Butterball has to stay outside and so can you."

Not bothering to reflect on the fact she was talking to the dog like a person, she let the screen door slam behind her before quickly stepping outside to make sure Dog hadn't taken off at the sound.

Relief swept through her to find him still there, his snout resting on his paw. "Good. Stay." Turning back inside the house, she quietly closed the screen door, but left the solid door open. She'd only be a minute anyway.

Striding into the kitchen, she rummaged through the cabinets for a bowl to use. Not sure how Annette would feel about a dog using one of her soup bowls, Riley pulled a plastic Toy Story bowl that Charlotte used and filled it with water. Logan could always buy his daughter a new bowl though it was more likely Annette would take the opportunity to shop for her great granddaughter.

She dunked her finger into the bowl of water and grimaced. It was lukewarm. That was a problem in the Arizona deserts. Getting cold water out of the faucet was an impossibility except in the winter. Glancing at the refrigerator ice dispenser, she made her decision. Setting the bowl beneath it, she pushed the handle and ice clunked into the bowl sending water splashing everywhere.

Great. It was only water. It would dry. She hit the handle again and more ice poured in.

What about food? Had Dog eaten? Did Whisper literally just pick him up off the side of the road and come straight to Last Chance, or had she fed him something on the way? He didn't eat the rat, but that could mean he simply had good taste.

Opening the fridge, she scanned the contents. Her gaze caught on the plastic container of leftover meatloaf. She took it out and set it on the counter. What if he didn't like it? Opening the drawers at the bottom, she found ham and turkey slices for sandwiches, along with lettuce, tomatoes and mushrooms.

Dr. Jenna had said that Butterball ate good dog food that contained protein and vegetables. There was no dog food in the house, but this was definitely protein and vegetables. Opening the cabinet where Annette kept her paper plates, Riley grabbed one and covered it with some of everything she found.

She took a few bites of cold meatloaf while she worked. When she'd filled the plate, she took a few more slices of ham and turkey and stuck them in a sandwich bag. If the dog was really hungry, she'd give him more. If not, she'd eat them. After putting everything away, she picked up the plate in one hand and the water in another. That wasn't going to work. Setting the plate down, she grabbed the sandwich bag and stuck it in her back pocket. Then picking up the plate again, she slowly walked back toward the front door.

Dog sat on the other side of the screen, his tongue still lolling out. She hoped this helped. She didn't want to be responsible for him dying. She couldn't handle anyone else dying under her watch.

She pushed the screen door open with her hip and set the bowl of water down on the porch.

Dog didn't move.

"Don't you want some water?" She crouched down next to it and swirled her finger in the icy liquid. She held it out to Dog. "It's cold."

He sniffed her finger and licked.

"Go ahead. Have some."

Dog's one eyebrow rose as he looked at her, then he moved his gaze to the water.

Whisper said to think of him as a little horse. She softened her voice. "Go ahead, little horse. It's all for you."

The dog moved forward and started lapping.

Triumph shot through her, and she barely kept in her shout. Instead, she slowly rose, but didn't dare move, afraid he'd stop drinking. This taking care of little animals wasn't easy. She'd take Cyclone over them any day.

At the thought of the Clydesdale, she swiveled her head to make sure he was behaving himself. Logan had used him to drag the lumber back to Cole's house just the day before, so Cyclone should be good until Sunday.

Dog licked her hand, bringing her attention back to him as he sat on his haunches in front of her.

She still held the dish of food in her other hand. Duh. "Are you hungry?" Crouching once more, she set the plate down. "I hope you like it. It was all I could find. Everything else is frozen." She'd need to thaw something for herself for tonight, or she could just eat potato chips and a melted provolone and mayo sandwich. "Go ahead, try it."

Dog sniffed at the plate before swallowing the meatloaf whole.

Crap, was that normal? He must be seriously hungry.

He sort of chewed the ham, but didn't eat all of it before turning to the turkey.

She moved to the closest porch chair and sat on the arm while she waited for him to finish. He hadn't touched the vegetables when he turned back to his water dish and drank some more. Two ice cubes got licked over the edge and onto the porch. When he finished, he walked to her and sat.

"Are you done?" She pointed to the plate.

His head swiveled to look where she pointed, but he didn't move. Instead, he faced her again and put his paw on her leg.

What the heck did that mean? "You still have more." She looked over him at the plate before meeting his dark brown eyes, that one eyebrow higher than the other again. Was it stuck there or…She didn't take her gaze from his as they stared at each other. She'd bet he wished she could read his mind. "Good boy?"

His tail waved slightly.

Was he really that desperate for praise? He'd never make it in the Army. "Good boy." She gave it more enthusiasm and the paw came down, the butt came up, and the tail wagged like the American flag in a sandstorm. She rose. "You know you could hurt someone with that thing?" She pointed to the still wagging tail.

Dog's mouth opened as if he smiled at her. She shook away the thought. Dogs didn't smile. Did they? She headed for the steps, and he bounded down them ahead of her. Pausing, she looked back at the half empty paper plate. Maybe he'd eat some later.

He ran across the packed earth of the parking area then back to her.

"Do you want to go for a run?"

He barked and sat, the eyebrow moving up though he

didn't close his mouth. It was the weirdest thing, as if he found her odd. She probably was to a dog that had a master who took care of him. Her heart tugged at the thought. And then that jerk of an owner went and dropped him on the side of the road. She knew what it was like to be alone in the world. "Come on. We'll go slow."

Turning, she headed for her horse. When she stopped by Domino, she was pleased to see Dog followed. "Domino, this is Dog." She grimaced. "Do I need to give you a temporary name?"

Domino lowered her head to a look at Dog then raised it again. For her that was acceptance. Dog sat as if waiting for the next command. He couldn't be that well trained, could he?

Setting her foot into the stirrup, she threw her leg over Domino's back and settled into the saddle. "You ready?"

Dog's butt came back up, the tail smacking back and forth as if ready for whatever she suggested. She clicked her tongue and set Domino into a walk. Dog trotted alongside...for about twenty feet before he stopped to sniff at a bush.

If she kept going would he follow? She let Domino continue then getting nervous as the distance increased, she called out. "Are you coming?"

Dog snapped his head up and bounded after them. Relieved, she grinned. "Nice to have your company."

Her relief ended fifty feet later when Dog bounded after a gecko on a prickly pear cactus, barking as the critter easily climbed between the needles. "Leave it be. Come on."

The barking stopped, but it took a few more minutes before the dog gave up and followed. Just as he came even with her, she urged Domino into a trot. As she'd hoped, he ran alongside, moving too fast to notice anything else. When they made it to Cole's, she took Domino over to the small barn and went inside.

There was a little fridge in the tack area, and she grabbed a cold water for herself then came back out to run the hose for Dog while Domino took advantage of the stop to drink water from the automatic waterer Cole had installed.

Once again, she studied the road to Last Chance looking for the new horses. Where was Garrett? He'd said he'd arrive in the morning. She pulled her cell phone from her back pocket and looked at the time. He had less than an hour left. He didn't seem like the type who would be late. Then again, she didn't know him.

She didn't need to know him either. Just enough to work together. Sure, he was nice to look at, but she moved around for a reason. Handsome or not, he was just a co-worker, like Trace and Logan. For all she knew, he had a wife, and that was just fine.

She looked longingly at Whisper's path through the desert. Waiting around was never her thing. Staying busy and productive had always been her way. Now, it was what kept her mind from wandering down dark paths she never wanted to go to again.

Back at the main house, the two stalls were ready for the new horses and all the animals were taken care of. She'd even fixed the rail Cyclone broke. There were other projects, but none she could do while alone. She hadn't painted the new rail yet. She could move a couple horses and do that...*if* Cole had bought more paint.

She snorted. She was ninety percent sure he'd forgotten, but it was worth a look. Striding back to Domino, she mounted up. "Come on dog, time to go back."

As he trotted toward her, she noticed dust on the road to the main house. Finally. She looked down for Dog and found him gone. What? "Dog!" Twisting in the saddle, she looked behind her. "Well, shit. Dog!"

He was halfway down Whisper's path, which let farther

into the valley, and he was racing like the hounds of hell were on his tail.

Turning Domino around, she chased after him. "Dog! Come here!"

As if her anxiousness at losing the small animal had communicated itself to her mount, Domino raced faster. She let her have her head as she turned off the well beaten path to follow dog across the Sonoran Desert.

She groaned as the jut of earth that was the back side of the entrance to the old copper mine grew larger as they approached. *He wouldn't.* "Come on, Domino. You can catch him." Her horse sped on.

Suddenly, Dog took a hard left and disappeared, but she'd finally seen what he was after—a jack rabbit. It had to be equal to him in size!

As she and Domino came around the side of the old mine entrance, her worst fear was realized. The dog had gone inside. "Fuck."

As her horse slowed to a stop, her palms became slick on the reins. She and Domino faced the dark entrance, fallen beams littered the opening. Those were the ones Cyclone was supposed to drag back to the house. She dropped the reins and wiped her hands on her jeans, but it didn't help. Her heart was racing and her body remembered.

She grasped the pommel and leaned forward. "Dog! Come heeeere." Her voice cracked, and Domino's ears laid back. Forcing herself to move one hand to her horse's head, she patted her. "Sorry, Dom."

Taking a deep breath, she stared at the opening. It was worse than a cave. It was smaller and already determined to be unsafe. Maybe if she waited, Dog would come back out. He'd eventually left the gecko alone earlier.

As if he knew she waited, a bark sounded from deep inside the mine.

Fuck. Fuck. Fuck. She had to get him out without going in. Gritting her teeth, she threw her leg over Domino and dismounted, but she couldn't move. Her feet felt cemented to the dirt beneath them. Cupping her hands around her mouth, she tried again. "Come here, Dog! Good boy!"

She waited as silence greeted her. The entire desert was still. The heat rose from the dirt as the sun baked down on it, all creatures safely in the shadows prepared to sleep the day away. Not even a hawk or buzzard moved through the sky.

She stared at the dark opening, memories rooting her to the spot.

The gunfire behind her let her know how close they were. One lucky shot had a bullet ricocheting off a boulder ahead of her. She needed to find a good place where she could pick them off, one at a time. But running uphill made her an easy target.

Another bullet whizzed by as she kept her head down while she weaved between the boulders that covered the sandy mountain. When the ground leveled out, she raced across it, her cover almost nil.

An opening in the ledge ahead was her best chance for disappearing. Not even hesitating before the tall, wide, almost white entrance of what was sure to be an endless tunnel system, she ran inside. The coolness hit her, helping her to think more clearly.

She rounded a corner and three darker openings greeted her. Choosing the one to the far right, she raced down it, the light getting dimmer and dimmer. Finally, she stopped and listened. Voices echoed off the cave walls, making it impossible to tell how close they were. All she knew was they were inside, and they were looking for her.

Chapter Four

Garrett slowed the truck, letting it roll forward a few feet down the road to Cole's so the trailer would be in the shade. A cloud of dirt in the distance told him the wind must have kicked up a dust devil in the valley. Turning the truck off, he jumped out.

He walked around the front of his vehicle and looked for Riley. A lone truck was parked near the house, and since it was the same one that was there two days ago, it had to be hers. Maybe she was in the barn.

Striding toward the structure, he stopped to give Black Jack a pat, the horse greeting him as he approached. The outdoor stall attached to the barn was actually the perfect solution for a claustrophobic horse. He had a new appreciation for the quirks of rescue horses. Stepping into the dimness of the barn, he noticed the ATV parked at the very back.

Listening, he heard no movement. "Riley? You here?" When silence greeted him, he moved forward. She must be in the house. Opening one of the stall doors where she said she'd put the new horses, he scanned it. She'd even added food and water. Guinness and Blaze would appreciate that.

He headed back outside, watching the front door as he strode to the back of the trailer. He didn't actually need Riley's help to get the two geldings settled into their new quarters. He just thought she'd want things done her way.

Unlocking the back, he lowered the ramp before untying the lead on Guinness. He was an American Quarter horse similar to Black Jack with a black mane and tail, but his body's color was much darker. Clicking, he walked Guinness out and led him toward the barn.

Lady, in the north corral trotted over and shook her head. Guinness didn't even see her, his focus on Black Jack as they moved closer. Garrett could feel the tension between the two horses as he walked Guinness into the barn. He'd let Riley know that the two may need time to get used to each other.

Once Guinness was settled, he returned to the trailer for Blaze. It was obvious why he'd been given that name, the blaze of white on his nose gave him a friendly appearance.

As he walked the horse toward the barn, Blaze pulled toward Lady, blowing air quickly out his nostrils, obviously excited to see her. She watched him avidly, her ears straight up.

"Not yet, buddy. Let her enjoy her alone time. Haven't you learned anything about females after all these years?" He chuckled as he patted the animal to redirect him. As they moved past Black Jack, Blaze tried to greet the other horse.

Not sure how that would go, he kept them separated, though his feeling was Blaze would acclimate a lot faster than Guinness. Once he had Blaze settled in, he strode back outside. Where was Riley?

He could leave the paperwork for the two geldings on the porch or under her windshield wiper, but he wanted to talk with her again. She was an enigma, and he didn't like enigmas. He needed to figure her out.

It was no different from when he was a curious thirteen-year-old and he wanted to know what Area 51 was really about.

It took months of research, a whole summer to be exact, but he'd concluded the government purposefully fueled stories of aliens to hide what they were really doing there. His hypothesis was it had to do with advanced weaponry, not all of which was successful. Since the government didn't want the public to know about either the weapons or the failures, it subtly encouraged the stories of aliens, staying completely silent on the true goings on there. Even as a teenager, he'd thought that a brilliant strategy.

But he doubted that Riley's closed demeanor was meant to instill curiosity in those who met her. Now knowing she'd been in the military, he had no doubt her persona was to cut questions off before they were raised.

Lifting the ramp, he slammed it shut, locking it while keeping his eye on the front door. Unfortunately for Riley, he was persistent, and despite questioning his motives for being so intrigued, he couldn't leave without talking to her again.

When she didn't come outside at the loud bang, his senses when into high alert. Something wasn't right. He had the same feeling when a fire was acting strangely. Sometimes it meant they were gaining control, but sometimes…

Striding to the house, he ran up the three steps to the porch, yanked open the screen door and banged on the closed front door. He focused on listening, waiting to hear footsteps inside, a yell, anything that indicated she was okay. When all remained silent, he tried the door. It was unlocked, which just made him more uneasy.

Entering the white hallway with wainscoting running its length, he quickly ducked his head in the two front rooms, but there was no sign of her. In fact, the house felt eerily empty. Visions of her lying on the floor unconscious filled his head. "Riley! You in here?"

Not waiting for an answer, he strode down the hall,

checking the kitchen, family room, master bedroom, sun porch on the back, even the half bath. Heading back for the stairs at the front, he yelled again. "Riley O'Hare! Where are you?"

Bounding up the steps to the second floor, he made a quick inspection of each of the three bedrooms and bathroom. Now that he'd ascertained she wasn't in trouble, he exited the house more calmly. Walking outside, he took stock of the area.

Her truck was here as was the ATV. So unless she'd taken off with someone, which was possible, though unlikely as she knew he'd be here with more horses, that meant she had to be on the ranch somewhere.

Movement in the south corral caught his attention. It was Lucky and Phoenix running between their mothers. Maybe Riley had gone for a ride. Stepping off the porch, he once more headed for the barn.

The only time he'd seen Riley soften was when she'd hugged her black and white paint. The horse wasn't outside, so was she in the barn? After a quick inspection, he had his answer. She had to be out for a ride.

Still, it didn't set well that she would ride out knowing he'd be arriving. Maybe she was at Cole's. It couldn't hurt to head out and check…but on which horse? Though the horses he'd just brought had no particular issues, his gut told him Wyatt would be pissed if he showed up and one horse was missing.

He had no doubt Wyatt would arrive within the hour if not sooner. He really needed to talk to Riley about the man before he arrived. Decision made, he grabbed a saddle and bridle and walked out to Black Jack. "What do you say, boy. Ready to stretch your legs?"

The fine horse's ears pricked up as he opened the stall and saddled him. In short order, they were galloping down the road to Cole's. When they arrived, he tied Black Jack to the small corral and looked around. He called out a few more times. The silence seemed to laugh at him. It had to be about noon and the desert was as silent as the dead.

Stepping just inside the smaller barn, he found Cole's two horses but no paint. Once again, the feeling that something wasn't right gnawed at him. Stepping back outside, he stared at the ground. He was better at tracking a fire than a person, but it couldn't hurt to try.

There were horse prints over tire tracks and they led toward the desert. Untying Black Jack, he followed the tracks. As he spotted a narrow trail, he noticed dog tracks as well. Had a rabid coyote been out here? As far as he knew, Cole had no dogs on his ranch, but he couldn't be sure.

He continued down the path. The tracks could have been made days ago, but he had nothing else to go on, except the feeling in his gut that it was important he find Riley, preferably before Wyatt arrived.

When the tracks veered from the path where fainter tracks could be seen continuing, he mounted Black Jack. "Let's take a walk." From on top of the horse, he could see the tracks clearly in the dust that coated the ground. He was lucky the wind hadn't wiped the tracks away.

The image of the dust devil he'd seen when he arrived bowled through his mind. What if that hadn't been a dust devil?

Riley forced herself to walk the fifteen feet that separated Domino from the entrance to the mine. It was like a black hole to hell. She stood before the opening no more than ten feet wide and seven feet tall. Miniscule compared to the cave she'd run into outside Chora in Afghanistan.

"Nope, not going there." She shook her head. She wasn't going into the mine either. She needed something to lure Dog out. Something more exciting than the damned rabbit. Food would be—she reached her hand into her back pocket and pulled out the baggy with lunchmeat. Score!

"Come here, Dog!" She opened the bag. "You want some more meat?"

No sound emerged from inside.

She tried again. "Come on, Dog. Aren't you hungry?" She tried to make her voice sound enticing, but being so close to the entrance had her throat too tight. *Come on, puppy. Don't make me go in there.*

Maybe she should go back to the ranch and see if Garrett would help. He should still be unloading horses.

At the sound of a yelp, she started, her heart moving into her throat. That didn't sound good. A rabbit couldn't hurt a dog. Did he misstep and even now was standing in the dark with one paw lifted? Or had a piece of the old shaft hit him and pinned him and that's why he wasn't coming out?

Even as the image of Dog lying unable to get up materialized in her mind, her decision was made.

Walking back to Domino, she grabbed the water bottle she'd dropped in the saddle bags and the towel she always brought with her. Then she checked her pockets as usual, stuffing the baggy back in her back pocket. "Wait for me, Domino. I'll be right back."

Returning to the mine entrance, she tried one more time. "Dog. Come here, Dog." Her voice barely made it past her lips.

Embrace your fear. Let it make you stronger, more in tune with your surroundings.

Her father's voice as he coached her while rock climbing when she was still a teen reverberated through her mind. If it could keep her alive in Afghanistan, it could keep her alive retrieving a mutt from an old copper mine.

Throwing the towel around her neck, she turned on the flashlight of her cell phone and stepped inside.

Just moving out of the sun had the air feeling cooler. As she stared at the blackness beyond the light, her throat completely closed, making it hard to breathe. She was Army dammit. As her father always said, *act like it*.

The ground was littered with both manmade and natural debris. Stepping over two of the old beams that used to support the opening, she moved her light over the wall and up. The header beam was missing, too. Nothing held the ceiling in place anymore. A chill ran through her, causing the sweat beneath her breasts and arms to feel downright cold.

The walls and ceiling were brown just like the dirt on the desert floor. Dirt that could be whisked away by a breeze. She swallowed hard, trying to free her throat to speak. She called out again. "Dog, where are you?"

A skittering sounded on her right, and she swung the light to the wall in time to see dirt settling on the ground. Great. Just great.

She remained where she was, listening, still close enough to the entrance to escape if the walls crumbled. But staying there wouldn't find Dog. "Come on Dog. Don't make me come after you." She kept her words quiet, pleased to hear no crumbling dirt.

Focusing the light ahead of her, she peered down the tunnel. The steel rails were still intact, though the wood supports were barely discernable, either covered in dirt or disintegrated. Based on how the Arizona heat dry-rotted the sturdiest items, she'd lay her money on disintegrated.

Standing where she was certainly wasn't going to solve anything, except to make it harder to move. Every one of her muscles felt tight enough to snap. Taking a deep breath, she counted to ten. On her exhale, she moved forward, staying between the rails, not willing to move anything.

Find Dog.
Dog needed help.
Dog couldn't find his way out.

She kept her focus on her mission, ignoring herself. That had always worked well. Retrieve dog and return to camp. Just the two of them. *There was no one else. No one left. All shot. She had to make it back.*

The brown earth without supports changed to brown earth with squared-off supports and then to a more narrow passage of hard rock in a mixture of grays that that curved to a peak not far above her head. She continued forward stepping carefully, listening intently.

Ahead the tunnel split, halting her forward movement. *This wasn't right. There were supposed to be three. She blinked, not comprehending.*

A bark came from the left tunnel. She shook her head as her brain cleared itself of old memories. Dog. She was here in Arizona looking for the dog. Grasping onto that thought with her mind, she moved closer to the entrance of the left tunnel. *It felt wrong. She wanted to go right. Right was where the hole to the cavern was that only she could fit through.*

No! This was *not* Afghanistan. Dog was in the left tunnel. "Come on O'Hare, hold it together." The sound of her voice helped her stay focused. "Dog, are you down there?"

A small woof floated up the tunnel followed by scratching and a whine. Was he hurt? "I'm coming. Don't move from there. Wait for me."

She started forward again keeping the light on the ground. Staying between the rails was easier now as less rot had occurred and the wood cross-ties made a fairly clear walkway. "I'm coming. Where are you?"

She lifted the light to peer down the infinite darkness,

movement at the very end of her beam catching her attention. She hurried forward, focused on the rump and tail of Dog. As she drew closer, she moved faster.

"Shit." Two fallen beams had left a small hole big enough for a rabbit to burrow through, but too small for Dog's hip bones, or she hoped it was too small. Dirt littered the ground around Dog as he wiggled to get through.

Dropping to her knees, she grabbed him with one arm, but as she pulled him back, he tried to get away, causing the beams to shift. Dropping her phone, she wrapped her other arm around him and pulled him back. The top beam slammed down on the one below it, closing off the hole.

Dog squirmed in her arms, but she held on until he licked at her face.

"Ugh, stop that. Gross." She let go one arm and wiped her face with the towel.

Dog barked.

"Ow, I'm right here." Grabbing her phone, she turned the light toward dog. He was dirty, but didn't appear to have any scratches. "The rabbit's gone home. You ready to get the hell out of here?"

Dog wiggled in her grasp, and she released him. He immediately turned back to the beams and sniffed.

"See, I told you. It's gone. Now let's go home."

Dog pawed at the wood.

"Oh, no. You are not digging under there. Come on." Bending over, she scooped him up again and headed for the exit. Even with her phone light on, she couldn't see it. Her heart thudded as her memories threatened to play with her head.

She grasped dog tighter. "We're in this together." Last time she was alone. Now, she had Dog and an open exit. She just needed to get back to it. "Okay, you weren't that far down here. It's probably only a quarter mile at best. Stay with me here."

She was only talking to keep her own sanity. "There are plenty of other rabbits out in the desert for you to chase, and I'm sure when Whisper comes home, she'll introduce you to all of them. Though I doubt she'd be happy if you decided to bring one home less than alive. She's very particular about her wildlife. No, you don't qualify as wildlife."

Part of her was glad no one else could hear her. "I may be insane talking to you, but it's better than going bat-shit-crazy in this crappy mine. As soon as we get back, I'm making it a priority to board this hellhole up."

As they exited the rabbit tunnel where it connected to the main one, she halted. Now it looked like two tunnels, one to the right and one to the left. She turned the light back toward the ground to see if she could see her footsteps. She wasn't sure, but it looked like a possible print to her right. Removing the towel from her neck, she walked back the way she came, searching for an outcropping in the rock. Finally finding one, she hung the towel on it. "There. Now if I choose the wrong direction, I'll know this was the tunnel where you went down the rabbit hole."

Moving back to the intersection, she turned the light beam to the ground. The last thing she needed was to twist an ankle on her way out. She was almost there. She had to be.

"Riley, you in there?" The loud voice sent dirt skittering down the walls.

Her heart jumped in her chest. "Shhhhh." Great. Now she had to deal with Garrett, too. How had he found her, and why wasn't he at the ranch with Wyatt?

"Riley?" More dirt hit the ground.

She snapped. "Will you be quiet! Can't you see this mine

is unstable." At her words, a fallen timber ahead of her shifted from where it leaned against the wall and fell, slamming onto the rails, the force vibrating the ground beneath her feet.

Fuck! She started to run, no longer caring about being Army. She wanted out!

Footsteps coming toward her made her stop. *They found her! She spun to run back the way she came.*

"Riley." Garrett's quiet voice, stopped her.

She turned back to see a light like her own. What was she doing? This was Arizona. Grasping Dog close, she started toward the exit again. Light meant escape.

It took her a few moments to understand the light was from Garrett's phone, but it didn't matter. He'd come from outside. She had to get outside.

The light came up and shone in her eyes. "Riley?" He was only a few feet away now.

She stopped, turning her head. "Mind not blinding me?" She blinked as white spots danced against the darkness.

"What the hell are you doing in here? It's not safe."

She wanted to laugh and lash out at the same time. Instead, she did neither. She headed for his voice even as she watched the ground beneath her feet. When she came abreast of him, she continued to walk past, but he grabbed her arm.

She yanked away from him, losing her balance and hitting the side wall. Her phone dropped, but she still had Dog. Panic crept up her throat as she slid to the ground, dirt trickling beside her, and she closed her eyes as memories of being hit with pounds of earth flooded her psyche. Her breath caught, and she shivered with fear.

"Hey, you okay?" His deep voice above her pulled her from the brink of terror.

She nodded, but didn't open her eyes.

"We're not that far from the exit. You ready to get out of here?"

More than ready, but she couldn't seem to open her eyes. "Minute." The word rasped from her dry throat.

"No rush." He didn't touch her, but she could sense him close.

Now all she had to do was open her eyes and walk out. She wouldn't have to crawl out, just stroll outside into the Arizona heat. Just open her eyes and...and stroll. She could do that. She was Army. Act like it! Despite her pep talk, she couldn't make it happen.

Would he think it weird if she asked him to guide her out? But let him know her weakness? She'd never let her men or women know she was afraid, and that was when she had reason to be afraid. This was all in her head. All she had to do was open her eyes and walk.

Dog came to her rescue, sort of. At that moment, he decided her face being that close to his was entirely irresistible, and he licked her cheek.

Her eyelids rose as she turned her head. "Will you stop that?" Her gaze landed on her phone on the ground, its clear case reflecting the light from Garrett's. She snatched it up.

"Need help?" He kept the light out of her eyes, but she could see his outstretched hand beneath it.

"No, I'm good." That would rank right up there as one of the most bald-faced lies she'd ever told. She wasn't good. She was a mess.

Grasping Dog tighter, she rose and looked toward what she thought was the way out. There was no light, just darkness. Had she mixed up again and lost her bearings? Her heartbeat raced as dread slithered up her spine. "Where's the exit?" Her voice squeaked, her hysteria just below the surface, but she didn't care. She had to get out.

"It's right up there. No need to worry. Here, let me turn off my light."

Her breath stopped as they were enveloped in darkness, but as her eyes adjusted, she could see the reflection of light off the cave walls up head. She breathed in. There must be a bend in the cave she hadn't noticed. Without thought, she moved forward and promptly tripped.

The hand on her upper arm kept her from going down. "Hold on, let me give us some light."

She didn't need light, she needed to get out. She took another step just as light speared the ground in front of her. *At the sight of the bulge in the dirt, she shifted her footstep to avoid the IED and bumped into her escort. God, the bombs were everywhere! How could she have missed them on the way in?*

"Riley, stop."

At the commanding tone, she regained her balance, but she couldn't obey. She didn't care if she was dishonorably discharged. "I can't. I have to get out."

"Okay, okay. Here."

The ground beneath her feet lit up again, and she started forward, careful to avoid the bumps in the earth, staying between the lines of the path. Had she seen those when she ran in? As she came to the bend in the cave, the heat and light from outside streamed in. The opening was bigger than she remembered digging, but she didn't care. She was getting out. She was free!

She hugged herself tightly and a loud yelp issued out. *She stopped, confused at the animal in her arms, her mind trying to grasp her reality.*

She had no time to contemplate where it came from as a loud creak filled the cave followed by a deep rumbling. Rocks rolled down the walls as two large beams crashed across her path. Dirt showered from the ceiling like a waterfall, the light from outside disappearing.

"No!" She lunged forward.

Like a slingshot, she felt herself pulled backward and she lost her balance, falling.

"Oof."

She didn't think twice about the body beneath her. Just another dead enemy, but the exit! Scrambling up, she stared at the blackness in front of her. Blocked.

Buried alive…again.

Chapter Five

Garrett rubbed his side where Riley's elbow connected as they fell. The dark mine was eerily quiet after the cave-in. Not even the dog he'd seen in her arms made a noise. The only sound was heavy breathing coming from directly above him. "Riley?" He kept his voice low, not wanting to scare her more than she already was.

She didn't answer.

Concern had his mind racing even as he slowly stood. He knew panic when he heard it. For such a tough woman, something about being in the mine had seriously freaked her. It could be the darkness, claustrophobia, or even a fear of paranormal spirits. It was a rare mine that hadn't seen at least one death, and from the looks of the age of this one, it had seen more than a few.

Again, he kept his voice low like he would when one of his men were hurt. "Riley, it's okay."

The crunch of dirt was his only warning as she spun toward his voice. "Okay? Okay? Sure. Everything's just fucking fine. Dying in a cave is just what they want. Isn't that how you always pictured you'd go?"

"They?"

She laughed, but it was a far cry from real. "Personally, I

expected a bullet through my head or child bearing presents in the form of a grenade."

Understanding dawned. The cave-in must have triggered an episode from when she was overseas with the military. Damn, had Cole said where she was? He racked his brain, but came up with nothing.

Slowly, as not to startle her, he crouched down and searched for his phone. As his hand brushed it, the light, which was still on, streamed across the ground.

She pounced, trying to wrestle the phone from him as if it were a gun, and he was intent on shooting her.

"Riley, stop! It's me Garrett." He wrenched it free and turned it on her.

She held her arm over her eyes and lunged for him.

He easily side-stepped her rush. Would she recognize him? Quickly, he turned the light on himself, careful to shade his eyes so he could still see. "It's just me, Garrett." When she didn't attack him, he risked shining the light against the ceiling to spread it over them.

She stood absolutely still, her chest heaving from her exertion, her brows lowered in confusion, her hands curled into fists. But it was her eyes that rooted him to the spot. They stared at nothing until she lifted her gaze to his. His stomach tightened even as he broke into a cold sweat. He'd seen that look before…on a corpse.

What would shake her out of it? Something important. Her horse? No, the paint was outside, patiently waiting for her, and she was stuck in here. The dog? "Where's your dog?"

For a moment he didn't think it had worked, but then she blinked. "Dog?"

"Yes, the dog you were holding?"

She glanced around the immediate area as if she couldn't move. "Dog? I don't own a dog."

"He's a little white thing with brown spots. He licked your face."

Her eyes widened, and she spun to look behind her.

Damn, now she thought the dog was buried. He hoped not. "What's his name. I bet he ran into the tunnels with all the noise."

"Dog." Her voice came out in a whisper, completely defeated.

He had no clue what the hell he was doing, but his gut told him he needed to get her back into the present, such as it was. Turning away from her, he yelled. "Hey dog. Come here, boy."

A whine greeted his call and relief flooded him, though the whine was concerning. "Come here, boy." He gave a whistle, which sent small stones cascading down the cave-in behind him.

"Don't." The word came up on him in a hiss. "The dirt is still unsettled. The ceiling could go."

He looked above where they stood, his light revealing rotten cross beams. She had a point. The sound of soft footsteps came closer, and he shifted his beam back down the tunnel.

Suddenly, Riley brushed by him and crouched down as the mutt came into the lighted area. She scooped him up and stood, turning around to face him. "This is Dog."

He squelched a chuckle. "Dog? That's his name?"

She turned her head away as the dog tried to lick her face. "He's not mine. He was abandoned and Whisper found him on the side of the Carefree Highway. She was on her way to Vegas, so she told me to take care of him until she comes back. He doesn't have a real name."

He nodded as if that all made perfect sense. He supposed for Last Chance Ranch it did, he simply hadn't worked there long enough to know.

Her gaze moved past him, and she stiffened as if seeing the cave-in for the first time in the present. "We're trapped."

He glanced over his shoulder. "Maybe, maybe not." He brought the light down and focused it on the ground, taking the steps to the cave-in. Slowly, he moved the light across the newly blocked tunnel. "It can't be that bad. We are very close to the exit." He finished his examination then turned to face Riley when the silence lengthened.

She stood there staring at the wall of earth behind him, the faraway look back in her gaze. "Riley."

"They won't leave right away."

He strode right up to her, breaking her view. "We're in an old copper mine outside Phoenix, Arizona. No one is out there except your horse."

At the mention of her ride, she blinked. "Domino?"

"Yes. Now why don't you take Dog and sit over here." He led her twenty yards farther down the rails to where the walls turned to solid rock to take her mind off the blocked exit, scooping up his cowboy hat on the way.

She sat on the ground with her back against the wall, her knees pulled up and the dog settled against her chest. It made him think of his niece and her blanket. She wouldn't go anywhere without it. Riley's hand absently stroked the dog's back.

Not sure how long her mind would stay in the present, he looked around for anything to dig with. It may be a mine, but from the looks of it, it was well over a hundred years old. Mining copper and other precious metals in Arizona had changed significantly in the early 1900's. This was definitely 1800's.

He scoured the ground. Finding her dropped phone, he handed it to her before continuing to search the immediate area. He didn't want to go too far from her in case she reverted back into the past again.

A rotten rail tie was the best he could do. Pulling it from

the dirt, he moved to the bottom of the cave-in and set his phone on the ground with the light shining up and started to dig.

"Stop!"

At the sudden shout, he stilled. Looking over his shoulder, he found Riley staring at him hard. "Why? Don't you want to get out? I need to see how thick this pile is."

She shook her head. "You don't dig at the bottom. You dig at the top, as high up as you can go. Digging on the bottom will just cause the new earth to fall on top of you."

That made a certain amount of sense. "How do you know that?"

She didn't answer. Instead, she shifted her gaze to the dog and remained silent.

Letting her rudeness slide, he rose and started to pull loose gravel from the top, but the more he pulled the more seemed to take its place. "Damn." Frustrated, he threw the wood aside and looked around the dimly lit area. At least they had some light thanks to his phone.

His phone! They could call. "Well, hell." Picking it up, he looked for a signal.

"It won't work."

He shined the light above her head. "What won't work?"

"Your phone. There's no signal here."

Did she have an answer for everything? "You don't know that. I might get one if I move to the right spot." He started to walk around the area, watching for the signal. Maybe he'd get lucky.

"The closest base is over an hour's drive. Can't expect help from them even if I could reach them. It was just a routine trip. No one was supposed to die."

He stilled at her words. She'd slipped back into the past, and his gut said that wasn't a good place for her. Maybe all she needed was some hope. "I'm sure someone will come looking for us. It will be pretty obvious we aren't there with our vehicles parked outside."

"No." Her tone made it sound like she'd given up. "They took them. Valuable assets. Good for an ambush. It worked on us."

A chill ran across his skin, very similar to when he called for his men to move back from a fire line, but was it due to a present threat or from her past experience...or was it her?

He didn't respond to her, more determined than ever to find a signal. After fifteen minutes of trying every possible place, he finally admitted defeat. "There must be too much earth around us."

"No, there would be no signal even if we were outside. It's no man's land out here."

He strode toward her. "We may be outside Phoenix, but Last Chance isn't off the map. Wickenburg and Canterbury have doubled in size just in the last five years since I lived here." He stopped in front of her and waited to see if his words would register.

She didn't move for a long time, but finally she looked up at him. "The signal only reaches Cole's house because he put in a booster. This valley is a dead zone."

Relief combined with irritation at her know-it-all attitude. Giving up, he sat down next to her, his back against the wall. They needed a plan of attack. "You seem to know what won't work. Any ideas on what will?"

"Turn your phone off. You'll use up the battery."

Swallowing a curse, he did as she suggested. The cave became absolute blackness. He lifted his hand, but couldn't see it. It was even worse than the old days when he worked on structure fires and couldn't see crap due to smoke. There was something absolute about the darkness that made him uncomfortable. "Now what would you suggest?"

"Take stock. What we have, what we need. Set a plan. Implement the plan. Failure means the plan needs to be reworked. Create a new plan. Repeat until there is success. There must be success."

His unease ramped up at the monotone quality of her voice. It was like she'd been brainwashed and repeated the message as taught. "Where did you learn that? In the military?"

He sensed her movement. "My father."

From the sound of her voice, she'd turned her head toward him. "Was he in the Army?"

"Air Force."

When she didn't continue, his irritation returned. The last thing he wanted to do was play twenty questions in the pitch blackness.

"Senior Master Sergeant O'Hare made sure I was well-equipped to succeed."

He wished he could see her face because her tone didn't give him a clue if she was happy about that. He was pretty sure his own father was more excited than even he was when he graduated with his fire science degree. "Then you've followed in your father's footsteps. I bet he's proud of you."

Her strange laugh was back. "No, he wasn't. I went into the Army. He never said it, but I know he felt betrayed. He died on his fifth deployment."

He let out a low whistle. "I'm sorry. That sounds like he was gone a lot."

"It was better than staying home, at least that's how I looked at it."

He didn't know what to say to that, so he waited to see if she'd reveal more. The silence stretched out to what seemed like a half hour, but he imagined it was only a few minutes before he spoke again. The total darkness was disorientating.

"I followed in my father's footsteps as well. He was a firefighter. He—"

"Did he die in a fire?"

Surprised by her question, he answered quickly. "No. He retired. He says he'll probably die from my mother's cooking because he just can't stop eating it." He smiled into the darkness. "My mom can cook."

When she didn't respond to that, he had to assume that she wasn't interested. That was fine. He just wanted to keep her in the present. "So your father said to take stock of what we have and what we need. I think all we have right now is our bare hands and that won't get us out of here. We should explore the mine and see if there isn't something we can use to dig with."

"Digging with our hands will take too long. I have one lip balm, a packet of ibuprofen, mints, an SOG pocket knife, a bandana, a bottle of water, and some sandwich meat."

His brain skidded to a halt. "You have all that?" He frowned in confusion. He hadn't seen a purse on her.

"Yes." She wasn't facing him anymore. He could tell because her voice wasn't as strong.

While it was an impressive stash for being trapped in a mine, he didn't see any of it being relevant. "None of that will help us dig our way out of here."

"No, but it will help us stay alive. What do you have?"

Good question. "I have the clothes on my back. No, I also have my wallet, a pack of gum, a pocket knife, and a handkerchief."

"That's acceptable. Our knives could come in handy for eating and the gum and mints will help us stave off thirst as long as possible."

"You have survival experience." He ground his teeth. Not the smartest thing to say to someone who kept drifting back in time.

"Yes." The single word came out in a whisper.

Again, he had the feeling that he needed to pull back and this time he listened to that feeling, his curiosity be damned. Obviously, she'd survived and was using what she'd learned now. "How long have you had the lunchmeat with you?"

"Since about eleven-thirty. Why?"

"We better eat it now. It will be rotten soon if it's not in a refrigerator, and though it's cooler in here than outside, it's not that cold."

"You're right. I forgot. What I wouldn't do for some MREs right now."

He could hear her moving around. "Why do you have lunchmeat on you? Were you planning a picnic."

"No, I was trying to feed Dog. I have turkey and ham left. He doesn't like ham. You can have that and I'll split the turkey with him."

He wasn't going to take more food than she had, so after a brief negotiation, they split it evenly among the three of them. After eating his share, he got back to what she'd said earlier. "We know what we have, so next on your father's list is to determine what we need. I'd say a shovel would be convenient."

"Break it down to the elemental components. We need something to move dirt."

"Besides our hands."

"Yes."

Again, her voice softened. He wanted to ask if she'd had to dig her way out of a situation like this, but the words stuck in his throat. Whether from caution or not wanting to know, he wasn't sure. At least if they determined they needed to move the earth with something besides their hands, he had an excuse to turn his light back on and search the mine tunnels.

Standing, he powered on his phone again and turned on his light. The brightness after such complete dark actually hurt his eyes, and he aimed the phone down the tunnel to lessen the intensity.

"What are you doing?" She set the dog on the ground and rose.

"I'm going to search these tunnels to see if we can find something to dig with. I doubt we'll find an old pick ax still intact, but iron of any kind could help." When she didn't argue with him, he started back the way they had come when he found her.

Should he leave her there or would she wander off and back into the past? He halted. "Are you coming?"

Riley stared at the black void beyond Garrett's light. Her body seemed to heat up from the inside out, causing sweat to build up along her neck and beneath her breasts. The ceilings were so low, like the back of the cave she'd been buried alive in, the very back.

Hold it together, soldier. This is Arizona, not Afghanistan. They may both be hot, dusty, and start with an A, but they're far different. For one thing, the only danger here is Mother Nature, and maybe that hot cowboy with the cute ass.

Okay, now she was definitely losing it. "Of course. Come on Dog. Since you like this place so much, you might as well lead the way." Dog, who had sat next to her, picked up his butt and wagged his tail. "No, I'm not going to get that rabbit for you. If I find that rodent, we're all eating well tonight."

She started forward, ignoring Garrett's wide eyes. "Well, let's see what we can find. Your phone battery won't last all day."

His gaze scanned her as if to make certain she was okay then he faced forward. Did he realize how easy it was to read him? Then again, he probably never had to hide how he felt. It was an odd thought, and she shook it off.

They continued forward. When they drew closer to the fork in the tunnels, she snatched Dog up, not in a hurry to have him get caught between boards while trying to find the stupid jack rabbit. The fork came into view and again, she had the urge to go to the far right only the third tunnel she wanted wasn't there.

Garrett halted. "You and Dog came from the left. Did you see anything down there?"

She hadn't exactly stopped to smell the roses. She'd had one thing on her mind, get Dog and get out. She stifled a snort. Look how well that turned out. "Nothing that I noticed while searching for this mutt."

"Then let's go to the right."

She nodded, marveling at how calm she was. Maybe now that her worst fears had been realized, she had nothing left to fear. *Except starvation, dehydration, and being shot when she exited.* She shook her head, to get rid of her poisoned thoughts.

"Yes or no?" Garrett stared at her, his brows lowered. He was either confused or thought she was crazy.

She'd put her money on crazy. "Yes, let's go to the right. I just had Dog's hair in my face."

"Okay." From the sound of his voice, he didn't believe her, but he turned around and started down the mine tunnel.

A smile threatened. The man had no clue that she was the last person he wanted to be stuck in a cave with. Mine! She was in a mine. An old copper mine. *Fucking-A, Riley get your shit together. This is not a cave. The ceilings are too low, there are rails on the ground, and there's only two tunnels.*

Right. She knew that. The cave outside Chora, which had

at first been an escape, had become her tomb when the bastards had blown the entrance to bury her inside. The destruction at the wide opening had been complete, the debris yards deep. This was a simple cave-in.

But it *was* the same. She was buried alive, again. The calm she'd recognized only minutes earlier evaporated as her gaze swept the sidewalls, instinctually searching for the small hole she'd squeezed through as the Taliban scoured the cave. *It had to be here. She must be close. She'd only run for a hundred yards or so. Or did it just feel like that? She listened for sounds of pursuit, but the only sound was her own footsteps and those in front of her.*

She halted, but the footsteps continued, taking her light with them. Quickly, she ran forward again, desperate to find the hole. Excited arguing sounded in her ears, back toward the entrance. Maybe they would shoot each other. It had happened before.

Suddenly, a flash of light reflected off the cave walls, and she dove to the ground, covering her dog, protecting it.

Dog? She blinked as the animal licked at her face.

"Are you okay?"

The male voice above her sounded concerned. That wasn't the voice she'd heard behind her. Releasing the dog, she rolled over to get her face out of the dirt. Quickly, she shaded her eyes from the bright light. "Who?"

A man crouched down next to her. "It's me, Garrett. Are you hurt? Did you trip?"

Garrett.

Arizona.

Mine.

Shit.

"Yes, I tripped. Help me up." She lifted her arm.

He stood and helped her stand. "Did you twist an ankle or anything?"

She brushed off her jeans then walked in a small circle to make it more believable. "Nope. I'm good." She looked around. "Where's Dog?"

Garrett scanned the area with his phone to find Dog sitting just ahead of them as if he waited for them to go deeper into the darkness. "Come here, boy. I don't think we need to go further."

"You don't?" She crouched down to encourage Dog since he didn't seem inclined to move. When he trotted over to her, she felt an odd sense of pleasure. That was silly.

"No, I don't think so. Take a look at what I found."

She scooped up Dog and moved to where Garrett stood in front of what looked like a small room carved out of the side of the wall.

"It's an old ore cart. The wood is worthless, but the metal pieces might help with digging." As Garrett moved the light over the rusted, decaying wooden cart on wheels, a reflection of the light flashed.

She dropped to a crouch out of habit. Shit. She lowered her head as if inspecting the workings beneath the cart. What the hell had caused the flash? All the metal on the cart was rusted over. "I'm not sure we can get this apart." She rose again.

He looked at her oddly. "I was thinking of these side pieces." He focused the light on metal bars that made a V on the side of the cart. "If we can get the rivets out, they might work."

She continued to scan the cart, looking for what caused the flashing. "That would take too much energy. We need to conserve that for digging. Are there any spare parts in here?" She squeezed between the cart and the side walls of the little room. There were old carbide cans, what looked like the sole of a shoe, and a couple small timbers. Now those might come in handy.

When the cart suddenly moved and the light lessened, she plastered herself against the wall, holding Dog close.

Garrett stepped back in. "That should help."

She relaxed and watched the ground as the light moved over the room going past then coming back to rest on a pile of what looked like metal bars.

"Now these could work."

"What are they?" She stepped closer to examine the bar in his hand.

"Rail spikes. They used them to anchor the track for the mine cars. It's not a shovel, but it's better than using our hands."

Before using her hands again, she'd sit and wait for death. That was if she didn't totally lose her mind by then.

"Too bad there's no old shovel or pick ax in here." He continued to sweep the room, even shining the light on the ceiling.

Another flash hit her and she crouched again. "What is that?" Irritation flooded her at her involuntary actions.

He moved his gaze to her. "What is what?"

"Those flashes? Your light is reflecting off something."

"I think it's a mineral in the stone."

"Well, stop it."

He walked over to her. "Do the flashes bring back memories?"

She nodded, hating to admit that she couldn't control her own body. She could almost see her father laughing at her.

"Then let's get out of here. I'll grab some spikes and we can see how they work."

She rose slowly, thankful he didn't comment on her weird reactions.

He picked through the stack as he judged each one for its strength and ability to move through dirt. She moved out of the small space, not comfortable with how tight the quarters were with two people in it, though it could make the perfect spot for a bathroom.

The cave she'd been buried in outside Chora had wide tunnels and high vaulted ceilings. The mine tunnels were barely five feet across, and the ceiling in some places was only high enough if she walked in the middle, the rock walls forming an arch.

She shivered, thankful for Dog's little body warmth. Everything about the space was cold, harsh, and unforgiving. Even in the light, it was nothing but greys and whites with a few brown lines through it to break up the monotony. At least the cave had been all hues of brown, or as they used to call the scenery then, a whole lot of "blah." Right now, she'd take blah over the mausoleum they were in.

Garrett stepped back into the narrow tunnel just in front of her. "Okay, let's head back to the entrance and see what damage we can do. According to my phone, we still have a good half a days' work we can get in." He started forward, his stride like that of most cowboys set on a particular task.

The irony of his words hit her sideways. "Yes. We want to finish up our work before dinner's ready. Then we can see what's on television or stream a movie."

He halted, and she barely stopped herself from running into him. As it was, she lost her balance and stumbled back a step.

He turned and held up the spikes in his hand. "And if we're lucky, these will make that possible. Don't assume the worst."

She lowered her brows and stared at him. Where the hell did his optimism come from? Did he not understand that they were buried alive with no one to know they were missing for days? Sure, they could last that long, if, and it was a huge "if," the cave-in could be cleared without the rest of the tunnels imploding. Had he noticed the cracks in the walls and the layers of loose rock in between what looked like solid rock?

"What?"

"Nothing." She shrugged her shoulders. "If we're going to do this, we should do it now, while we're healthy."

He nodded before turning around and striding forward. "I don't plan on getting sick anytime soon, but you're right. While we have the energy, we need to get as much done as possible."

She followed him in silence until they arrived at the sight of the cave-in.

"Here, hold this." He handed her his phone and two spikes.

She set Dog on the ground. "Once you get into position, I'm turning off the light."

He frowned at her. "How am I supposed to see what I'm doing?"

"You're not. The dirt will follow gravity. It's more important to save the light for when you need it." She looked at the phone's battery life. "You only have about twenty-five percent battery left. You need to use it wisely."

He didn't move. "Why do I have the feeling you've done this before?"

Because I have. "Just start digging. If you're lucky, light from outside will let you know when you're close."

"I hope that's sooner rather than later."

She did too. The opening was much smaller than her cave, but that could mean that the earth would be more compacted and harder to get through. Then again, since it wasn't sandy, maybe that would help them and it wouldn't refill in again.

Just thinking about the constant sand caving-in her progress every night had her palms sweating all over again. She'd had the nightmare of being buried in loose sand for months. If she hadn't been able to use the trickle of water she found in the cave to wet down her own tunnel walls and ceiling to form a harder surface, she would have died. Only thirst had driven her deeper into the caves, but in the end, it had saved her in more than one way. Without that life-giving water, she would have simply disappeared from humanity.

And no one would have known. No one would have cared. Just another military statistic.

Dirt falling down the pile in front of her brought her out of her morose musings. Garrett used the spikes to pull dirt away and down the mound. Since he was in a steady spot, she moved the light toward the ceiling, over the wall behind him to the ground at her feet, letting his eyes slowly adjust. Then without warning, she turned it off.

He didn't say a word, but the sound of rocks rolling down to lay on the mine floor continued. The sound was familiar yet different. It was odd to hear it and not be the one causing it, but it wouldn't make sense for both of them to work. They didn't need a wide opening, just one big enough for a single person to crawl through. When he was tired, she'd do her part.

Slipping his phone in the front pocket of her jeans, she took one spike in each hand. These would have been less helpful in Afghanistan, but still it would have saved her hands. The remembered pain caused her breathing to hitch. This was Arizona. She needed to remember that.

As something brushed against her leg, she jumped back. "What the hell?"

A low whine issued forth.

"Dog, what is it?"

He didn't say anything else, but she felt his body against her leg as he sat on her foot.

"Really? Don't tell me you're afraid of the dark. You're the one who ran in here in the first place."

The drizzle of dirt stopped. "So that's why you're in here."

The sound of Garrett's disembodied voice startled her. She kept thinking she was alone. "Yes. He saw fit to chase a jack rabbit in here."

The dirt started to trickle down again. "Did he catch it?"

"No, but he wouldn't come out. When I found him, he was halfway through an opening into a hole that had been boarded up. After I pulled him out, the wood fell. I don't think that rabbit is going to get out of here either unless he has some secret burrow that tunnels through the mountain.

"I doubt a critter like that would run into a mine unless he had an alternate exit."

Garrett's voice, coming out of the blackness like it did, was soothing. It was a deep baritone with a calm cadence. Had it been like that when he'd dropped Lady off at the ranch? Funny, how she didn't notice things like that when she had her sight, but the second she'd turned the light off, her other senses slipped into overdrive out of habit. Now if she could just keep her mind focused on her—no their—current situation, she might just make it out without losing her mind.

Yeah right.

Chapter Six

Garrett kept his motions even, hoping he'd make a bigger dent by staying focused in one area. He didn't have an issue with the dark, but he'd never been in this absolute blackness. It was like having his eyes closed but they were wide open. He could feel himself straining to see something, anything. He couldn't even be sure he was digging in the same area, relying mostly on the position of his arms to his body.

On one hand, he understood the need to turn off the light. On the other hand, he didn't want to waste effort by digging wide when he could be digging deep. Now that Riley had stopped talking, he was less sure of his movements. Her voice was a directional beacon.

He stuck the spikes in front of him and paused. "I noticed when I pulled up with Guinness and Blaze that only your truck was at the ranch. Will Cole be back soon?"

"No."

At the sound of her voice below him, he started moving dirt again.

"Cole's gone for the weekend. The soonest anyone will be back will be Sunday night, unless Lacey and her mother-in-law get into an argument."

There went the hope someone would be looking for them.

"Damn, Wyatt is going to go off the wall. He probably has already."

"The grandson?"

He nodded before remembering she couldn't see him. "Yes. He was maybe an hour behind me. At least I moved the horses into their stalls before looking for you."

"I don't care how off the wall he goes as long as he takes care of *all* the horses. I was going to be the only one at the ranch all weekend. With me here, there's no one else to feed them. I hope he has enough brains to do that much."

"I wouldn't worry about that. He'll probably take care of them and then give us a piece of his mind when we finally get back."

"If we get back."

At her soft-spoken words, he paused again. "Of course, we will. Cole will come looking for us. My truck and trailer are sitting in the yard and neither of us is there. They'll find us eventually if we don't get out of here before then. I just hope your horse is smart enough to go back to the ranch." He'd been surprised to see the black and white paint eating grasses nearby, its reins dragging on the ground.

"Oh, Domino is smart, but she won't go back. She'll stay outside as long as I'm in here. There's no water out there." The concern for her horse came through in her voice.

"All horses return home at feeding time."

She sighed, the soft sound floating up to him in utter defeat. "No, she won't. I told her to wait. She won't leave. She may wander to eat, but she's very well trained."

She may think her horse would stay, but he knew from experience, survival would trump training every time. Except when stubbornness got in the way, which just proved he was dumber than a horse.

Shaking off the thought, he focused on his movements, striking the spikes deep into the loose gravel and pulling them toward himself and over to the side. But the quiet didn't help. She was obviously perfectly happy sitting in pitch blackness with no sound whatsoever. He'd never met a woman like her.

"I rode Black Jack to look for you. I thought you'd be at Cole's." He waited to move the dirt, anxious to hear her voice. Not only did it keep his directional focus in place, it also assured him she was still in the present.

"That's where I would have been if not for Dog here."

He could almost hear her stroke the dog, but it had to be his imagination. He shoved dirt aside. "If I'd known you were at this old mine, I wouldn't have saddled Black Jack."

A soft chuckle came from the darkness below. "He threw you."

"Not exactly, but he sure as hell tried." He'd been so focused on the paint standing in the light shade of the Palo Verde tree that he hadn't seen the entrance to the mine before the horse. Black Jack had reared, almost unseating him. He had to jump off the horse as it came down. "Then he hightailed it back to the ranch."

"I'll bet he's shaking. Whisper will have your head if she discovers you rode him out to the Take a Chance mine."

He crawled forward about a foot and stabbed the dirt with the spikes. "I'm sure once she knows I came out here to find you, she'll get over it."

A snort floated up behind him. "Not likely. If it comes to a decision between a person and an animal, Whisper will choose the animal every time."

And he always chose lives over homes...until he didn't and paid for it. "That sounds like her values are a bit mixed up."

"I don't know. She hasn't had the best experience with humans. She's even friends with a mountain lion."

The two unrelated statements told him two things. One, the darkness may be getting to her as well, and two, Last Chance may do more than rescue horses. It sounded like it had rescued people, too.

"Are you making progress up there? Is the sand filling in as soon as you move it?"

Sand? "No, the gravel must be staying because I've been able to move forward." Though it was true, he wasn't sure it was actually progress. "Why don't you shine the light up here so I can make sure I'm headed in the right direction."

The sound of her boots scrapping on the dirt was a clear indication she'd been sitting on the ground. When the light came on, she had it facing away from him. Still, it seemed bright after the pitch blackness. If he had turned on the light, he would have had it shining directly on where he was working and probably blinded himself. Had she done that on purpose or just happened to face it that way?

She directed the light toward the ceiling, brightening the area where he was working without directly shining it on the spot. He'd been right. He had made progress, staying in the right direction, but it was minimal. He'd cleared a space about two feet wide and two feet high and only a foot deep.

She stepped out from directly behind him to view his handwork. "That's better than I expected. I thought for sure the ceiling would fill in the space you're creating. The entrance to the mine is so soft, which must be why they used beams for support. Back there," she pointed back into the mine. "If it caved in, we'd probably just have to remove the rubble and crawl out."

"Lucky us." He thought his progress was pitiful, but without a shovel, it was the best he could do.

Almost as if she read his mind, she spoke. "It's going to be really slow. I can search the mine further to see if there's anything else we can use."

That would be a good use of time, since they both would be doing something to get themselves out, but then he wouldn't have her voice to anchor his direction. Or, they could both explore, but would that be wasting time? Based on the depth of most mines, there should be plenty of air for them, as long as there weren't multiple cave-ins. And he was still positive Cole would get them out of there before they starved to death.

The light left as she turned. "Come on, Dog. There's got to be more tools in here somewhere."

"Wait." He scrambled down as a new thought occurred. What if she slipped into her past again or became lost? He'd only been inside one old mine, but if he hadn't had a guide with him, he would have never found his way out. "We're not following your father's advice."

At her confused look, he reminded her. "Your father said after we find what we need, we should make a plan. We didn't do that."

"And if it fails to create a new plan until achieving success."

As she rattled off the end of the litany, he relaxed. Keeping her grounded should help. "When I was digging, your voice kept me going in the right direction. So if we continue to dig with these," he held up the two spikes, "then one of us should remain here and keep talking while the other moves the dirt. If our plan is to gather more tools then we should both search, but this plan hasn't failed yet. I don't think I've been at this thirty minutes yet."

She glanced behind him before looking down at his phone in her hand. A smirk lifted her lips. "Fourteen minutes."

"That's it?"

"It feels like a lot longer in the dark."

The statement, said with such surety, gave him a chill. Again, he sensed that she may have been in a similar situation before, but what could cause her to know about working in complete blackness? Was it from crawling in tunnels in the Middle East or further back? Did her parents lock her in a closet or something? Even at the thought, his grip on the spikes tightened. Shit, he hoped he was wrong. "Why don't we continue working on this plan before we jump to another."

She gave a curt nod. "I agree. We can take turns. Every hour, we can switch off."

Relieved that she wouldn't be wandering off, never to return, he lifted the spikes. "Then I'd best get back to it." He gave his words a miner's drawl, or what he hoped sounded like one.

She didn't respond, simply lifting the light to allow him to see his spot on the pile.

"If you stay directly behind me and talk, it will help me keep on target."

She looked down at Dog. "We can do that."

Interesting. She included the dog. He had a feeling this Whisper wouldn't be getting her dog back when she returned at the end of the weekend. Turning, he climbed up the pile again and stuck his spikes in. "Ready."

The light shifted away to the far wall then dipped as she sat down. It moved again, telling him that Dog, must have decided her lap was softer than the ground.

"Really?"

At the sound of her disgruntled voice, he knew he was correct, so he kept his position. "Leave the light on a moment. I want to see how the dirt is falling." Pulling the spikes toward him and to the side, he watched the gravel fall to the mine floor. He adjusted his movement by twenty degrees and did it again. That was better. "Okay, I'm ready for my hour."

No sooner had he said the words than the light went out. He gave himself a half a minute to adjust to the blackness again and started digging. "You're going to have to keep talking.

"I don't talk much."

Now why didn't that surprise him. "Well, you do now." Stab. Pull back. And push. Stab. Pull back. And push. "Riley, I'm not hearing anything."

"What am I supposed to talk about?"

Adjust. Stab. Pull back. Push. "Anything. How about Last Chance?" That should be something to keep her in the present.

"Fine. I can tell Cole I gave you the employee orientation."

Stab. Pull back. "He really has one of those?" Somehow that fit his former co-worker.

She snorted. "Oh yeah. Complete with history of every rescued horse, though I don't think he actually writes those."

"Who does?" Push. Stab. Pull back. Push. Stab.

"I'm not sure. Maybe Lacey. She keeps everything straight on the financial end. You're required to know what everyone does, who the current horses are, where to order the grain and hay, how to get purchases approved, what kitchen privileges you have, and what to do in case of a fire."

At the last, he laughed. "Now that sounds like Cole."

"How did you meet? You don't seem as uptight as he is nor as forgetful."

Again, she attacked Cole. What did she have against him? "You don't like Cole, do you?"

"What?" Her immediate response accentuated her surprise. "Why do you say that?"

Stab. Pull back. Push. Stab. Pull back. Push. "You criticize him every chance you get."

"I do?"

He didn't feel the need to answer. Let her think about it for a minute. As it turned out, it didn't take a full minute, from what he could tell.

"I never thought about whether I like him or not. He's my boss, and as a leader, his skills come up short. That's probably why you thought that. Leaders need to take charge and delegate. Cole has liked things his way too long, and right now that doesn't work. He was promoted to Captain and married all in six months while trying to run Last Chance. He can't do it, but he won't let go of the reins."

Ah, so that's why Cole wanted him to work at Last Chance. "What about you?"

"What about me, what?"

"Why don't you take over as foreman and hire another hand."

"Not a chance in hell."

He grinned. She definitely didn't mince words. He liked that about her. "Why not?"

In the silence that followed, he wasn't sure if she was suddenly deliberating how to couch her sentiments or if she wasn't sure if she would answer. He continued digging. If she didn't speak again soon, he'd have to get her talking again.

Finally, she let out a soft sigh. "Been there. Done that. Not doing it again."

He adjusted his pull back. "Done what?"

"Had men under my command. It doesn't matter how knowledgeable you are or how well trained. Simply because I'm a woman, every decision I make is questioned. And then when the situation is critical and you could use some opinions, you get no input at all."

Her voice trailed off, bitterness and regret heavy in her tone.

He looked back from habit; the blackness was complete. He'd never had the experience, but he understood it. He'd seen female captains in the fire service struggle with the same issues. He'd even caught himself questioning an order, though silently. He was too well trained to vocalize any doubts. "When did it matter?"

She gave the odd laugh she had. It seemed to issue from some silent self-loathing. "When it didn't. A simple errand into a local town. Supplies. Nothing more than supplies. Not worth three lives."

The monotony of her words reminded him of her tone just before the cave-in. She was slipping back. He needed to ground her. Kicking himself for asking a stupid question, he pushed the gravel extra hard.

"Hey, I thought you were trying to get us out of here, not bury me alive."

He took a deep breath. He hadn't meant to hit her, but if it kept her from retreating into the past, he'd do it again. "Sorry. Lost my direction. So, what do I need to know for this orientation of Cole's?"

As Riley explained what he should know about Last Chance, he could tell when she found a topic boring or when it was something she strongly believed in. It was also obvious that she respected Annette, Whisper, and Jenna. She didn't seem sure about Lacey and Cole's soon-to-be sister-in-law, Hailey.

But when it came to the men at the ranch, she had very particular ideas. She thought Trace smiled too much, Logan was too focused on his family to be much help and Dillon had antiquated ideas about women. As for Annette's husband, she gave him a pass because he was old. It made him wonder what she'd think of his family.

"Okay, off." The dog shook himself before the scrape of

her boots told Garrett she'd risen. "Time's up. My turn." She switched the light on, again facing it away from the mound he sat on.

As his eyes adjusted, he swore. "This is pathetic." Despite all the gravel he'd moved, it didn't look like he'd made any forward progress, though there was a bit of a dip in the depth. He stabbed one spike into the dirt and pulled it back and away. More dirt filled the space from above. "We may need another plan."

Riley looked up at the dent Garrett had made in the mound of dirt. For an hour's worth of work, it wasn't much, but she'd seen worse. "Let me have my sixty minutes then we can reassess."

He looked doubtful, but clambered down anyway, bringing more dirt with him. "It feels like the whole mountain is in that one spot."

"We may just need to wait for it to settle down and pack itself in. You know, in about three years?"

Garrett stopped brushing off his jeans and gave her a grin. "Was that a joke?"

She rolled her eyes. "Of course, it was."

He shook his head. "I think that's the first funny thing you've said to me since we met."

What? Was that true? She'd never considered herself the life of the party, but she did have a sense of humor. Had she lost it back in that cave three years ago? Uncomfortable with the thought, she lowered her brows. "Let's see, I had Cyclone wanting to break every board in sight last time I saw you and now we are trapped in a cave, I mean, mine. I guess there hasn't been much reason to joke."

He shrugged his shoulders, but his grin remained.

She was thankful he didn't remark on the fact that she decided to joke while trapped underground. Turning, she took a step toward the mound.

"Wait. Let me have the phone."

Of course. She stretched her arm out, the light pointing at the ground. His hand covered hers for a moment before grasping the phone. It reminded her that she wasn't alone this time. If she could get out of her last entrapment by herself, she must be able to get out of this one. Feeling more like her confident self for the first time since she rode up on Domino, she returned her attention to the pile in front of her.

It was very loose gravel, much like the sand she'd dug through in the mountains outside Chora. But it *was* different. It could be packed hard and tight. She'd see what she could do. Getting into position with her two spikes, she stabbed them into the ground and pulled back the earth, sending it to her side. She watched as more gravel filled in.

As if he'd been waiting for her first dig, the light went off and she was back in the pitch black. At first, she didn't move, letting her eyes adjust to the lack of any light. Then she stabbed at the earth where she'd seen it fill in. Stab, wiggle, tug and shove out of the way. It was a familiar yet different motion. Last time she'd had only her hands to dig with. The spikes she held were sturdy and strong. She liked the feel. Leaning forward, she stabbed the spikes in again.

On her third strike, she felt her direction falter. Time to take advantage of having a partner in her predicament this time. "Did you fall asleep on me already?"

"With all the noise you're making, not a chance."

She snorted. "Good. So, talk." Stab, wiggle, tug and shove.

"What would you like me to talk about?"

She shrugged even if he couldn't see it. "Whatever. I

probably won't be listening. Like you said, just a directional cue." Tug and shove and stab.

Instead of being insulted, he chuckled. So much about him reminded her of the men at her outpost, but then he did something like that. "You said you fight fires for a living. Tell me about that." Wiggle, tug.

"That would definitely put you to sleep. I don't do that anymore, so it would all be me strolling down memory lane. I'll tell you about my family."

Great. Now she'd get to hear how functional his perfect family was. She'd lose track of his words in no time.

"As I said, I followed in my father's footsteps. My younger brother did in a different way. I became a firefighter and then a Hot Shot. My—"

"You fought wildfires?" That, she hadn't expected. That was seriously dangerous, not that house fires weren't, but wildfires were huge. Just a few years ago, a bunch of Hot Shots burned to death when the fire surrounded them. She'd seen it on the news. She'd just arrived in Arizona and it was all anyone could talk about.

"Yes, I did. My brother at first became an EMT before deciding to become a nurse."

Tug and shove. Stab, wiggle, tug and shove out of the way. "Not a doctor?" He was right, it helped to have someone talking behind her.

"No. He said doctors were, pardon the expression, assholes."

She smirked into the dark void. "Don't pardon yourself around me. I've heard it all and yelled half of it at least."

"That's right, you're Army. You know what it's like to have to watch your mouth around your mother."

Actually, she didn't, but then again, she hadn't respected

her mother. The woman was a weak emotional mess from day one. She stabbed the spikes in hard, wiggled and yanked them back, getting dirt all over herself. "Shit."

"I know. When I visit my parents, I spend three days practicing to keep my curse words under control, even if I'm alone. It's hard when you drop a twenty-pound bucket filled with cement mix on your toe."

Oh, she knew what that felt like, but she never kept herself from cursing. There was no point. Stab, wiggle, and tug. "What were you doing with cement mix?" *Just keep talking so I can get this out of my way. Shove.*

"I bought a fixer upper in Wickenburg recently. The cement was for around the posts I put in for a porch. I managed to get them in straight, but that's as far as I've gotten. It's really a two-person job."

She set each spike to the side of her and leaned forward to pack down the dirt in the small concave area she had so far. *This would help her judge her forward progress. The entrance couldn't be more than a dozen feet away if she remembered correctly. Of course, she'd been running at the time, so it might be farther, but twelve feet was a good number to start with. It made it seem doable. She just needed to keep twelve in her mind, not three. Three killed. Three times four was twelve. She would rest every three feet to honor them. What kind of honor was that? A moment of silence? What good did that do—*

"Everything okay up there. Need the light?"

The voice startled her and she froze. Who had found her?

"Riley? Is something blocking the way?"

Garrett. She let out her breath. She was in here with Garrett. "No. Just judging the distance." Crap, she needed to hold it together. She pressed her hands against the sides of her little tunnel before finding the spikes again. "You're right, it's easy to move, but it does like to fill in. I'm just packing the sides to get a better feel in the dark. Keep talking. Tell me about your place."

As he began describing the deal he got, she stabbed the spikes in. Wiggle, tug, shove away. He could act as her safety net. If she stopped sending gravel down the slope, he'd bring her back. More comfortable with that realization than she should be, she listened to his voice, though she didn't pay much attention to the words.

Every inch was an inch closer to freedom. She had tools this time to move the debris. This was natural, not caused by a grenade launcher. The cave had been forcefully closed, and it didn't want the blockage any more than she did. Shit. If this was natural, did that mean Mother Earth was reclaiming her space? She pushed the thought away. Earth didn't have a mindset. It was all in her head. *Just dig.*

Stab, wiggle, tug and shove it out of the way. She adjusted her position and continued. She was making good progress. It was so much easier with the tools. She paused again and padded the bottom and sides. Yes, she was making headway. It just took patience. She'd had to exercise far too much patience with her men, even with the one other woman in her unit.

As she shoved more dirt out of the way, silence greeted her. "Hey, you're supposed to be talking."

"I asked you a question."

"Ask again. I was concentrating." Obviously not on what he was saying. Getting out was more important.

"I asked you where you're from. Where's home?"

"I don't have one. I'm the only one in my family who's left, so wherever I lay down at night is home." And it was far better that way. No guilt. No responsibility. Except Domino. *Go home, Domino. Don't starve on my account. I'm not worth it.*

"I'm sorry. Was it just you and your parents?"

She shoved the next batch of dirt hard. "I thought you were the one talking."

"You really don't like talking about yourself, do you?"

"Is it that obvious?" Her voice dripped with sarcasm, but she didn't care. Her past sucked, and she didn't need to talk about it, no matter what the Army shrink said. Her present wasn't so great at the moment either, and she had no future plans.

"Blatantly. So Dog, what can you tell me about Riley. She doesn't want to hold up her end of the conversation."

Despite how ridiculous it was, she found herself listening as if Dog would tell him something.

"Really? Now that I didn't expect."

She stabbed the dirt hard. He was making shit up. The dog couldn't tell him anything. The dark must be getting to him. The first time she'd been buried, the darkness didn't matter because she was happy to have the Taliban offensive on one side of the closed cave and herself on the other.

"Very interesting. I'll be sure to remember that."

She pulled back and shoved the dirt to the side again. *Her mother was so fucked up. She'd never survive the darkness.* "Have you gone completely nuts on me. You're no help if you go crazy. You're just an added burden. I can't hold us together if you can't even function." She leaned far forward and stabbed the ground hard.

The voice that came out of the dark was soft. "I'm doing my best."

"Well, your best isn't good enough. Go get help. Go to AA or something. You need to be there for Carly. I don't know when I'll be deployed again."

"Riley."

She stamped down the small tunnel she made with her hands. "Don't Riley me. I'm not the one who's an emotional mess, you are. You need to pull yourself up by your bootstraps and save your daughter."

"Riley!"

"What?" She pulled back lifting her spike in the air, ready to strike.

"Who are you talking to?"

She blinked. That was Garrett. What the hell? She'd been talking to her mother. Shit, it was just like in Afghanistan, but that was after days of being alone in the dark. She'd only been in here a couple hours and not alone. She needed to get out.

She ignored Garrett's question and went back to digging. Stab, wiggle, tug, and shove. Stab, wiggle, tug and shove. She repeated the words in her head with each motion. Though the silence continued, she wouldn't ask him to talk. She just needed to get out.

Stab, wiggle, tug and shove. Pat it all down. Is that where patty cake came from? What was a patty cake? *Any cake would taste good right about now. She was low on supplies and if she didn't see daylight soon, she'd starve to death. Even if it was nighttime, she'd know. She'd feel air movement, maybe even see the stars. The stars were so clear here. It had surprised her when she first arrived to see such beauty in such a war-torn country.*

Pull back, pat down. Ignore the numb fingertips. Progress was paramount. Escape was necessary for survival. Whatever it took to survive. The beetles, the snake, the poor bird stuck in with her. She had to survive. Had to tell her superiors of the ambush, of her men shot down for no reason. No, there was a reason. They were Americans. They had a vehicle and that was reason enough.

What the hell were they doing over here. They all should go home. Not in body bags. She had to stay alive to tell their tale. She had to dig. Dig faster. Survive long enough to get out. Pat it down. Pull it out. Move forward. Get out. Get—No!

The swooshing sound of the collapse was not enough warning.

She spit out dirt, trying to breathe, the weight on her back pinning her down. The dirt suffocating her, covering her body. She couldn't move. Survive! Survive!

Chapter Seven

The sound of falling gravel had Garrett lunging forward in the dark, the phone forgotten in his rush. "Fuck! Riley!" He scrambled up the pile and latched onto her ankles. Throwing his body weight back, he yanked hard. She came out of the collapse coughing as they both lay on the slope of fresh earth.

"Are you okay?" He rolled onto his knees and feeling for her shoulders pulled her up so her face wasn't in the dirt.

She didn't respond immediately as she hacked.

He rubbed her back, patting it in between, keeping her torso upright despite the slant they sat on. His own heart was pounding a path out of his chest, and he focused on taking deep breaths even as he held her steady.

"I'm alive." A cough followed her pronouncement.

Unable to stifle his relief, he hugged her to him. "Thank God."

She pushed away, but held onto him. "What? Are you afraid to be alone in this mine by yourself? Worried about ghosts?"

He shook his head despite the fact she couldn't see him. "Yeah, that must be it."

"I thought so." Another cough followed her statement.

"Let me help you down."

"We're not down?" The softness of her voice said far more than her words.

He didn't blame her for fearing another collapse. "Only half way." He turned her forward to get her bearings and they half-slid, half-walked the last few feet of the slope. "Stay right here."

He moved to where he hoped the phone would be and instead found Dog. "Hey buddy, were you worried. She's okay."

"Dog?" At Riley's voice, the mutt moved, most likely to go to her.

He felt around until he finally found the phone and switched on the light. Damn, he'd blinded himself again. He quickly turned it toward the depths of the mine and looked back at Riley.

She fought off Dog's anxious licks. "I'm okay, you silly dog." She finally grabbed him and set him on her lap.

Her red hair was brown with dirt, her face filthy, and her jeans covered, but it was her left arm that concerned him. A six-inch scratch was deep enough to ooze significant blood. More than he was comfortable with. She had all the ingredients for an infection. "Where's that water you said you had?"

"We should wait. It's too soon yet."

Ignoring the fact that she sounded like there was a particular timetable they had to follow to survive, he pointed at her arm. "Not to drink. I need to clean that or infection will set in." And the last thing he needed was for her to become delirious.

She looked at her arm. "I didn't even feel that." She pointed with that hand, her other arm holding Dog at bay. "It's about ten yards down this tunnel on your side. There's a gray rock with an edge just wide enough for it and my phone."

He smiled at her before heading in the direction she'd pointed. "Gray, huh?" All the rocks were gray.

She shook her head at him, obviously not finding his question humorous.

He focused the light on the wall until it glinted off the plastic water bottle. Gabbing it up, he turned and headed back. "Don't let him lick that scratch. Dogs' mouths are filled with germs."

She frowned. "I wasn't planning to let him near it. I'm not stupid."

He slowed. "I'd never think you were stupid. It's just my firefighter training coming into play. It keeps the fear at bay."

"Fear? Of what?"

He sighed as he dropped down to his knees next to her. "Fear that you almost died. Fear that this might become infected and you get seriously sick. I always fear for those I save. It's why I jumped at the chance to fight wildfires, to avoid structure fires as much as possible. Structure fires could mean trapped people. Fear. Now keep Dog away while I clean this."

Pulling his handkerchief from his back pocket, he dribbled water on it and carefully cleansed the scratch. "I'd like to clean your whole arm, but that would take too much water. We should cover this to keep it clean. There's far too much loose dirt in here."

"You can use my bandana."

"Is that hidden somewhere, too." He glanced over his shoulder, his eyes scanning the wall.

"No, it's in my back pocket."

She rose and pulled out her bandana amid a spray of gravel. She held it out and shrugged. "Maybe not."

"We can leave the wound open, but only if you're careful not to lean it against anything."

"The only way I can guarantee that is to stand in the middle of this mine tunnel, and even then, dirt could fall from the ceiling."

She had a good point. He needed something clean. The outside of their clothes were filthy, but the inside might have possibilities. Unfortunately, all she had on was a tank top. He unbuttoned the end of his left sleeve, which was dark with dirt. "I'm going to need your help."

She buried the bandana in her back pocket. "Sure, what do you want me to do?"

"We need to rip this sleeve along the seam and at the shoulder. Then we cut off the ends, and—"

"The inside is a clean bandage. Got it." Reaching into her back pocket, she pulled out a multi-purpose knife. "Now, hold still."

He raised one eyebrow at her as he held the light so she could see the seam.

Slipping the sharp edge under the cuff so it faced out, she tore the stitching. Once started, she closed the knife and ripped the sleeve to the shoulder. "You know, it would be easier if you just took the shirt off."

That wasn't going to happen. At least not while the light was on. "We're almost done. If you're nervous about cutting me, you can hold the material while I do it."

She snorted, making it clear what she thought of that idea. Usually, a woman snorting to him sounded funny or vulgar, but Riley's snorts were done with such authority, it seemed like just another expression like a grunt or a whistle.

"There. Got it." The sleeve was pulled from his shirt in a final yank. "Nice guns. Didn't realize how much was under those sleeves."

He was glad she couldn't see his flush. "Good, now I can cut the ends."

She stepped back. "I can do it."

He had no doubt she could, so he let her finish the project.

"There. All ready for wrapping." She turned her left arm over to inspect it. Her movement had caused the blood to flow again. "Let me have your handkerchief."

Curious, he handed it over, holding the wet side in his hand. "This area is still clean."

Carefully, she used it to wipe up the blood, then she took the damp part and used it to clean more dirt from around her wound. When she finished, she looked at him. His surprise must have shown on his face. "What? Blood is moist and worthless at this point. Might as well save our water for staying alive." She held out the sleeve. "Your turn."

He stepped forward and took the material. "You better hold the light."

Now that he had a better view of the wound, he could see the jagged edges. Whatever rock had dug into her skin, it hadn't been sharp. Just sharp enough to do damage and possibly leave pieces of itself behind. He didn't like that idea at all. "Now that I see this more clearly, I should check for residual rock in the wound." He looked her in the eye. "It won't be pleasant."

Her strange laugh was back. "I'm sure compared to having all my fingernails ripped off, it will be a cake walk."

Assuming she wasn't serious, he ignored his own curiosity at the comment for expeditious treatment. By probing the wound and squeezing, additional blood with four small pieces of glittery rock fragments were extracted. Not once did she flinch or make a sound.

He held out his hand for his handkerchief, giving her a moment before touching her arm again. She handed it over without a word, her face stoic. Cleaning the wound once more with the small section of the material that was still useable, he stuck it in his front pocket and wrapped his sleeve material around her arm. Ripping the end in two, he tied it so it fit, but not too tight. Her arm needed stitches, but that wasn't going to happen before it started to heal unless they were miraculously rescued in the next five minutes.

"There, that's as good as we're going to get in here. We make a good team." He grinned, intending it as a compliment.

She didn't see him, too intent on her arm. "Looks good. So obviously that plan was a failure. I thought with packing down this earth, we could get farther, but it just delayed the inevitable. Any ideas?"

He stared unbelievingly as she took the water bottle he'd set on the ground and returned it to its place, Dog following her. She'd almost suffocated under pounds of rock and cut her arm badly but acted as if it was a minor setback. She was more than an enigma, she was as complicated as an unsolved arson investigation!

She sat down on the ground below her little rock-shelf and leaned her back against the wall of the tunnel. "Are you coming over here. I need to turn off the light. We've already used too much of it taking care of my arm."

"Sure." He strode over and plunked down next to her, still stymied by her reaction to what most would consider a brush with death and a painful aftermath.

His ass had barely hit the ground before the place went black again. The way she handled everything about their predicament screamed that she'd been in a similar situation before. He had to know. If it sent her back in time, he'd be right here to pull her back. "You sound like you've done this before."

"Done what?"

Good question. "Been trapped in a mine."

The silence was as absolute as the darkness. He'd count to a hundred and if she still didn't respond, he'd nudge her. He was on seventy-two before she finally spoke.

"If you mean, have I been stuck in a cave before, you're correct."

Damn. He let out a low whistle. "Obviously, you were rescued."

"Not exactly. No calvary came to my aid. They were all dead."

Her words had been spoken as a matter of fact, but the lack of emotion in her tone gave him a clue. Could it be the more monotone her voice, the more deeply she felt? When had she last spoken like that?

"This gravel is different. We're going to have to figure something out."

He shrugged out of habit. "Or we could just wait to be rescued. I don't know what time it is, but I'm guessing in about forty-eight hours at the most, someone will notice we're missing and start to search. With the right equipment, they could probably get us out of here in a couple hours."

"So, your plan is to just sit here and wait?" The shock in her voice was impossible to miss.

"It would keep any further injuries from occurring. We'll probably be hungry, but if we don't move much, we won't use energy. The temperature in here is comfortable, thanks to it being summer, so we could simply sit and wait."

In the deep darkness, he could hear her breathing increase. Did it scare her to simply wait? It grated on his nerves to be the one rescued instead of the one doing the extraction, but it did make a lot of sense in this case to simply remain still.

"No." The single word came out on a controlled breath.

He waited, expecting an explanation, but none was forthcoming. Fine. He wasn't excited about waiting either. For all they knew, if they moved three more feet of gravel, they could be free. "Good, that's not my style."

"Mine either. Then what are our options for digging out of here? We could look for another exit. That rabbit might have an escape route."

He shook his head. "I'm sure he does, but I doubt we'd fit through a rabbit tunnel."

"Well, it was a *big* rabbit."

Huh? She couldn't really be contemplating—

A chuckle sounded in the darkness.

More humor? It seemed odd coming from her, yet he had no idea why. "You mean like Alice in Wonderland? If so, I hope you have some of that special mushroom or we're going to get stuck."

"Not likely. Too bad Dog here couldn't sniff us a way out."

Something about her name for what looked like a Jack Russel Terrier bothered him. It was impersonal as if she wanted to keep it at a distance. Maybe she did, knowing Whisper would be coming back for it, but the chances of the animal being happy about that now were slim. "Don't you think you should come up with a real name for your dog?"

"Why? He's not mine."

"Maybe not, but even foster parents don't call the children 'boy' and 'girl' just because they won't be keeping them."

Silence greeted his statement.

Was she thinking of a name? "I've been thinking about getting a dog myself."

"Why?"

Her question surprised him. "For company. The great thing about a dog is its loyalty and unflinching desire to be in your presence."

"But you have to feed it and play with it and take it to the vet. That's a lot of responsibility."

Obviously, she'd never thought about being a mother. He'd

always wanted to be a father, but that wasn't about to happen now. Not since his last wildfire. "A dog is a lot less work than a horse and you own a horse."

"And because I do, I'm frustrated because I know she's standing outside this mine in the heat of the Sonoran Desert with no water."

For the first time he heard real fondness in her voice. "If your horse is as smart as you say, she will find shade and water when she needs it."

"I hope so. But if we can figure out how to get out of here, I can be sure she's okay."

"True. Then based on the gravel and your own experience, which is far more than mine in this situation, what do you think?"

"I think the gravel is too loose to hold up. We would need supports like were originally there. We'd have to dig enough to set up beams before the dirt caves in again."

He actually hadn't thought about reconstructing the tunnel, but if it was done on a small scale that might work. "That could work if we can find more timbers."

"There were a few in the side room we found earlier."

"True, but not enough. We'd have to explore farther and see if there were any more and do so before our phone lights give out." He didn't like the thought of being stuck in pitch black with no light available.

Her boots scraped the ground as she repositioned herself, at least he assumed that's what she did.

"And what if we can't find enough wood?" Her voice now faced him, validating his assumption at her movement. He liked that she faced him and turned to face her as well. "The only other option I can think of is to pull the fallen dirt into this space until enough has cleared for us to crawl out." He held up his hand as if to keep her from interrupting before he remembered she couldn't see it. Hell, even he couldn't see it and he knew it was there. He grinned at his own habits. "That is, of course, if the whole side of the mountain isn't in that pile."

"What we have going for us is that it's very close to the entrance, so even if it is the side of the mountain, it would only be up to a certain point. That's a lot more doable than a hundred yards into a complex cave system."

He wanted to ask, but right now was not the time. "Then our plan is to search for timbers and tools. Unless the Take a Chance mine ran along a short vein, my guess is there are a lot of tunnels to explore."

"I have no idea. Cole said it was originally a gold mine, but that was short lived and copper was discovered. I guess gold, silver, and copper hang out together."

That was one way of putting it. He was no expert, but if what she said was true, the split they found when they first searched could indicate an old gold tunnel on one side and the copper on the other. "If we can find the end of a tunnel, another room, or a major transfer spot, we might find tools and timbers."

Again, her boots scraped against the dirt. "Then we should get started."

Her voice came from above him, so he rose as well. "Let me get my light turned on."

Her hand on his chest halted him. "No. We know we have at least a hundred and sixty yards before coming close to the split. If we run our hand along the side wall, we can get there in the dark."

He didn't like that idea for more than one reason. First, it meant the pitch blackness would continue and second that she'd probably done the exact same thing once before. "That could be dangerous. We have rails and debris to navigate."

"We don't have to move quickly. It's not like we're on a timetable."

Her confidence bothered him. "There's a good chance we will be free of this place before our batteries run out."

"Maybe, but do you want to risk it?"

Shit. She was right. "Fine, but let me go first."

"Why? I've already been down this part of the tunnel twice."

It went against his grain for her to lead, mainly because that would be the most dangerous position. He tried to come up with a reason not to let her, but couldn't think of anything she wouldn't see right through.

"Ready Dog?" She grasped his shoulder in the dark and walked around him.

Not happy with the situation, he had no choice but to follow, her footsteps letting him know where she was. "I think Dog needs a new name."

"I told you, he's not my dog."

He shortened his stride, her voice closer than he'd anticipated. "That doesn't mean you can't give him a temporary name."

"Like what?"

He let his hand trail across the solid rock, occasionally disturbing loose granules as he stepped carefully. "How about Chance after the ranch."

"No. That could be confusing. Orphan?"

"That's just depressing."

She snorted. "What do you want, something like Precious, Snuggie, or Tinkerbell?"

He chuckled. "Definitely not. If he's a boy, it should be a male name. I noticed he has spots on him. What color are they?"

"They're more like splotches, like on a cow. They're brown, but not tan, more a reddish brown."

"What about Copper."

Her footsteps halted. "No, they're browner than that."

"I mean you could call him Copper like the mineral this mine was built to find. It's close to brown, plus he ran into an old copper mine."

She started forward again. "Copper? Hmmm. Hey Dog, do you like the name Copper?"

He squelched his own snort. Just then he heard her boot hit something hard.

"Ow. Damn rails."

He froze. "Want me to take the lead?"

"No, I'm fine. Just misjudged the spacing of the rail tie. We don't have that far to go."

And she knew this how? He had to admit she seemed a lot more confident in the inky blackness than he did.

Chapter Eight

Keep it together O'Hare. This firefighting cowboy already thinks you're off your rocker. No need to prove it by avoiding a snake that isn't there and tripping over imaginary rock formations. Keep the rock on your left and your steps measured. The only thing down here is rabbits.

His voice came out of the darkness. "I think we should stay to the left this time. See what's beyond where you found Copper."

Sounded like he'd decided on Dog's name. She actually agreed it was a good name. One she'd give the dog if she was keeping it. She'd tell Whisper that was the dog's name. The woman could always check with the animal to see if he liked it. At least, she thought Whisper could. Who knew for sure?

"Do you agree?"

Agree? Oh yeah. "Sure. One dark tunnel or the other, it's all the same to me." And that was the problem. It felt too much like the cave when there was no light. The only exception was the rail.

In Afghanistan there were miles of underground caves, some of which actually were said to have rails similar to this, but there'd never been any legit intelligence of that, at least not at her outpost. Maybe if she'd been on base like she was on her first deployment, she would have known more, but that first time she was too busy trying to train Afghans in US warfare to learn about any important intel.

The rock beneath her fingertips felt different, too. It wasn't nearly as porous as in the cave she'd been trapped in. Very few pieces flaked off and then suddenly many would. That's when she had a hard time focusing. Then it was too much like the cave. Even the ground burying her alive was like her first night in the cave. Except back then, she had no one to pull her out and she'd panicked. Even thinking about it had her heartbeat racing.

Deep breaths. She needed to take deep breaths because she could. Because Garrett had got her out of there and held her like she was important not to lose. It was probably just adrenaline from the sudden avalanche in the dark. Still, it felt good to be valued for a change.

"We should be about there." Garrett's voice coming from behind her almost earned him a swift kick to the gut, but she stopped herself in time, her action only getting as far as turning around. "Have you been counting steps?" She'd planned to but her thoughts wouldn't stay focused.

"Yes. I'll turn on the light and see if I'm right."

She looked away, so the light wouldn't blind her. She learned that trick quickly after the first time she turned on her cellphone light in the cave.

Reflected light filled the area, proving that Garrett had an excellent sense of measurement. A few more steps and they'd be entering the left tunnel of the fork.

He stepped around her. "We should pick up the pace while using the light."

Now he was the expert? She gritted her teeth to stop from voicing her thought. The man was helpful, and he wasn't bad company. She should be grateful he'd come looking for her, or she'd be in the mine alone with her thoughts…going crazy. "Then lead the way."

He strode forward a few paces into the tunnel then switched to the other side of the rails. "What's this?"

She looked at the wall and grinned. "That's my towel. I forgot I left it down here. I brought it in here with me in case D—Copper was hurt. On my way out, I left it here to make sure I was heading in the right direction." No need to let him know she'd felt completely turned around thanks to her past memories.

"Good idea. We can pick it up on our way back. If we need to change your bandage, it will come in handy." He started to move forward.

"I don't know. Copper licked my face when I found him, and I wiped it off on that towel."

He looked back at her. "Then no, we can't use it for that."

"But we can use it for toilet paper. I'll use my knife to rip it up."

"We may not be down here that long."

She kept forgetting that they could actually be rescued in a few days. "True. I'll just rip up half…for now."

Garrett nodded then resumed his direction, moving assuredly down the path the rail ties made, stepping on every other one.

Her stride wasn't the same at this pace, and she had to adjust every few ties, but it was still the easiest way to traverse the ground. The tunnel itself had very little room on either side, especially if she wanted to walk standing upright. They passed by Copper's rabbit hole, the dog not even noticing the boards blocking the spot. He was as intent on what was ahead as Garrett.

She, on the other hand, was starting to sweat. Her whole

body reacting to the knowledge that an entire mountain sat above her, and they headed deeper into it. *One well-placed grenade, a single mortar, an errant air strike, and she'd be buried under it, unable to breathe, unable to move.*

"I see something up ahead." His voice startled her. He spoke over his shoulder, his curiosity obviously peaked.

She blinked, keeping her gaze on the ties until she came right up behind him then looked ahead. "It's another juncture." That didn't excite her as much as it did him.

"Yes, but over here it looks like a resting place or maybe they switched carts out here, like some kind of transfer area." He moved to a hollowed-out section that looked like her old cave, though not as tall, but definitely wide. It was a large semi-circle with the rail going by it. It was filled with debris, specifically rail ties.

"These could work if we make our tunnel small." She picked a rail tie up off the four-foot pile. It fell apart in her hands. "Or maybe not."

Garrett stood next to her. "They probably dumped the rotten wood here. Let's see what else there is."

She followed him since he had the light. There was a very old coffee pot, half a pick ax head, a couple metal wheels from ore cars, what looked like suspenders, and an old lantern. Too bad they couldn't use that, but with no fuel, it was worthless to them.

"Hey, this would help." Garrett held up what looked like the head of a shovel, though there was no handle. He handed it to her.

What she wouldn't have done for one of these when she'd been in her cave. She probably could have escaped in far fewer days and with at least half her fingernails intact.

He pointed to the metal in her hand. "If we can find another of those, we could work together, making faster progress."

She stayed where she was as Garrett proceeded to make a thorough inspection of the items in the area, pushing things aside as he went. Copper followed him, sticking his nose into every nook and cranny he could find. Two rusted pullies fell off a pile of old wood and the dog jumped back. She pointed at them. "What did they need those for?"

Garrett stopped and looked back. "There must be a shaft or two down here. That's when they dig straight down to another level. They would hoist men and buckets up and down. Or it could simply be such a steep incline that they needed a rope to navigate it."

She shivered at the thought of crawling deeper into the mine.

He pointed to the floor next to the pulleys. "Some of these carbide cans are in better shape than the one we found earlier, but they're too small for digging."

"But they would be good for scooping." Compared to bare hands, anything was better in her mind.

"Scooping?"

She needed to remember he had never been buried before. "Yes. We're going to need a bathroom. The small room we found earlier would work well. It's a separate area away from the entrance where we should sleep. We can use the cans to scoop dirt to cover over our waste, keeping the smell down."

He studied her for moment. "Good idea. Here." He handed her two cans with no holes in them.

She had to admit, he did seem to value her input. In the Army she always had to be assertive to have her opinion heard. Garrett could make this soldier go soft. She set the cans next to the shovel head on the ground at her feet. Then dusted the dirt from the cans off her hands by brushing them on her jeans. "Too bad they didn't leave any gloves down here."

Garrett faced her, a dirty old hat in his hand. "This is thick leather. The winters out here must have been a lot cooler than they are today." He dropped it back on a three-legged stool that didn't look strong enough to hold the weight. "Ah, now this might work."

She waited as he pulled something from behind what looked like a pile of decayed straw.

He held the object up in triumph. "It's a metal pan for panning for gold. I wonder if this was originally the gold mining tunnel or if someone had used it for eating their lunch. Either way, it will work to scoop dirt."

"Good, now we can go back and get started again." She was ready to return to the entrance. *She'd rather contend with the darkness and know she was at the mouth of the cave than contend with the pressure of the mountain in the light. There was nothing of any use here. Whatever the cave had been used for before, it was long gone. From the marks on the ground, it may have stored ammunition and guns for the Taliban forces. It felt more than empty. The vaulted ceiling looked as if it could come down at any moment, like the one had in the other tunnel.*

What if she'd run to the far left instead of the far right? She would have been caught in that dead end. Would that have been better or worse than being buried alive? Her gut told her she was better off, but it was hard to count herself lucky. Was a quick painful death better than a slow painful one?

"There's just a few more feet to this area. I might find something better."

She dropped to the ground at the sound. They found her. How did they get through the cave-in? Her breath caught. Was there another entrance? Could she watch them covertly and discover its existence? No, she'd checked. There was nothing, not even in the ceiling. Then how did they get in?

"Riley, get up."

The command had her jumping to her feet. "Yes, s…" She swallowed her word. Fuck, she'd lost it again.

Garrett studied her as if he could discover what she was thinking. He didn't want to know. No one did. Other soldiers had experienced much worse.

"Let's head back. Why don't you give me the shovel head and you can take the carbide cans?"

A reprieve, but she doubted he'd let it go. Scanning the ground at her feet, she lifted the steel tool and nodded.

Garrett passed by her and led the way back in the direction of the entrance.

She wanted to tell him to turn off the light that they could feel their way back, but that would slow them down, and she wanted out from beneath the mountain more than she wanted light later.

When they arrived at the place she'd hung her towel, Garrett simply lifted it off the rock edge it hung from and continued on. They finally reached the spot where she'd left the water bottle. He halted and hooked the towel on another outcropping of stone.

She walked by him, but he grabbed her arm.

"Time to tell me about your last experience being buried under ground."

She jerked her arm free, unease filling her soul. "Don't you think our time is better spent digging out of this place?"

"No. I need to know what you went through."

And admit she'd been stupid, failed as a soldier, and now couldn't hold it together? Not likely. "Why. Once we're out of here, it won't matter anyway."

Dropping the pan, he put both hands on her shoulders. His grip was firm but not tight. "It matters now. I've seen a lot of trauma and no one has acted like you have. I need to know what you went through so I can be prepared. We're a team in here, and as a team we have to depend on each other. That means trusting each other with our very lives."

"A unit." She didn't want to be part of a unit. A unit meant friendship and responsibility and loss. She'd sworn off units.

"Yes, we're a unit."

She stepped back away from his touch. "No. This is temporary. You said so yourself. We'll be rescued." They would be rescued. People would know they were missing because they were part of a unit. She shook her head. No, she had to leave. She didn't want to be part of a unit, to have any connections.

Garrett wouldn't be put off. "Riley, look at me."

She forced her gaze to his. She couldn't tell the color of his eyes in the diffused grey light. What were they again? Blue? Grey?

"You need to tell me everything. It might give me an idea on how to get us out of here."

She snorted. "Not likely."

He continued to stare at her. It was the commanding look of a person in charge and it was hard to resist.

"What the hell position did you have in this Hot Shot force. Were you the commander or something?" She didn't hide the resentment in her voice. Obeying a command had been so drilled into her that she had a hard time ignoring his tone.

His lips quirked up. "Not exactly, but close enough."

"Just my luck." She stepped away again, but this time she walked toward the cave-in and glanced up at the rotten beams. "Right. I'll tell you the whole ugly story, but first we need to brace what's here. We can talk while we work."

"Now who sounds like a commander?"

She scowled. As a leader, she'd failed miserably. "I'm no commander."

119

"That may be, but you're right." He walked past her and scraped his fingers across the wood above his head. Slivers fell to the ground. "We didn't find enough timbers to brace a small tunnel, but there were enough to build a brace under this."

"Exactly." She examined the timber against the wall. "This is the last brace in the gravel before it turns to hard stone. Then we can pull back the cave-in dirt, covering the rails until we break through." Hope sang through her blood. They could do this. *And how many times had you thought that before and were wrong?* She ignored her inner voice. This was different. This was a mine and she had help.

She looked at Garrett who gave her a grin. "We have a new plan."

She nodded. "We do." As confidence filled her, she ignored the doubt that tried to creep in. They had a plan and this time they'd be successful.

Garrett sat down next to Riley against the cave wall that had become what he thought of as the staging area. He'd thought he was in shape after all the physical therapy he'd gone through, but obviously he wasn't near his old strength. Maybe Cole's idea of a weight gym in his station wasn't such a bad idea.

Then again, if he'd done as much work on his new old house as he'd intended in the spring, he'd be in better shape. But he'd felt restless ever since returning to the area. It was as if he had no idea what to do with the rest of his life. His goal had always been to be a Hot Shot. Once he'd achieved that, he'd thought he'd retire as one, but fate wasn't as kind to him as she'd been to his father.

"I'm wiped."

Riley's voice coming out of the blackness made him chuckle. "Glad I'm not the only one." Actually, he was relieved that he'd been able to keep up with her. She had obviously not lost any of her strength from being in the Army. She'd worked alongside him as they pulled the earth away from the pile and back into the mine, telling him about her work training Afghan soldiers overseas. She still hadn't told him about her last underground experience, but since she'd stayed with him in the present, he didn't push it, but he would need to know.

They'd made good progress with their new tools, but there was no sign of busting through...yet.

"It's a good tired. It will make it easier to sleep."

She had a point there. Though rail ties and rock would make for a difficult night's sleep.

As if she'd read his thoughts, she spoke. "I just need a few minutes rest, then we should make our beds."

"Make our beds? I noticed a number of items in that transfer spot down there, but a mattress was not one of them."

"No, but we have—ack! Copper, stop. Who woke you up? I'm going to change your name to Slobber if you don't stop licking me."

He grinned then reached over and pulled the dog off her. "Come on, boy. Settle down. You'll need to rest so you can help us again tomorrow."

A snort sounded in the darkness. "The biggest hole he dug was the one he took a nap in."

That was true. At first, Copper had positioned himself between them and started digging with his paws, but it wasn't long before he'd left them to dig somewhere else. When they'd paused long enough to recognize it was silent, he'd turned his phone light on briefly to find the dog laying in a hole he dug far away from them. Copper looked at them very proud of his accomplishment. He felt he should come to dog's defense. "Well, he *is* a small dog. And you can't really blame him for giving you kisses. You did save him as far as he's concerned." Heck, he would enjoy kissing her, too. Now where did that come from? That was a path he needed to avoid at all costs.

"I have a feeling he gives anyone he sees kisses."

She sounded disgruntled. One minute she didn't want to name the dog because he wasn't hers and the next, she sounded put out that he might like everyone equally. "No, it's just you. I'm holding him right now, and he hasn't tried to lick me."

"Humph."

Though it was said in disbelief, he could tell that she was pleased. Wow, sitting in the dark certainly enhanced other senses. He'd always known that in smoky areas, but even then, there was some visual context. "You were saying we have beds?"

"Right. Not beds exactly, but good material for them. In Afghanistan, we would swear at the sand, especially the sandstorms, but there were a couple occasions when I was glad for it. It acts like those mattresses that are touted on commercials. It conforms to your body.

He'd never thought of sand like that, but it made sense. That was the theory behind the old seventy's beanbag chairs that his great uncle used to have. "We don't have sand."

"No, but the gravel from the blocked tunnel is a hell of a lot softer than this rock. I'm going to bring some of it over here and build it up between the rail and the side wall. You may want to do the same on the other side. Then I'll use my bandana to cover my 'pillow'."

She was right. There was bound to be stones in it, but it would be better than sleeping on the rail ties. "That could work."

"I know it can. I just need a mint first. Are you ready for one?"

His mouth felt dry just at the idea of it. "Yes." While she dug into her back pocket, he contemplated his bed. Though she had a good idea of filling in between the rail and the wall, he needed a bit more room than that. He'd fill in between the two rails. It would also put him in close proximity if she slipped into the past again.

"Here. Drop one in your mouth from the roll."

He reached out to find her hand holding the mints. Doing as instructed, he managed to get one in his mouth without touching it with his filthy hands. What he wouldn't give for a dip in Lake Pleasant right now. He handed back the mints, and they slipped into a companionable silence.

It was odd to think that if he didn't return home tonight, no one would know. His family lived farther north and his former co-workers and friends were up there, too. The only people he knew in the area were his realtor, Cole, and some of Cole's station men from long ago when he'd worked there. The only reason anyone would look for him was because his truck and the Last Chance trailer were parked at the ranch house.

It was an odd realization that emphasized how disconnected he was at this moment in his life. Definitely not a feeling he liked nor wanted to continue too long. "Will anyone else be missing you tonight, besides Last Chance people. I mean do you call your mom every Friday or anything?" It was a long shot, but it would be good to know that Riley might be missed.

"Not likely since she's dead."

Shit, he stepped in it this time. "I'm sorry. You mentioned your father had passed. I didn't realize your mom had as well."

"It's not a big deal." He could picture her waving her hand in dismissal. "They're all dead. Dad was killed in Iraq, so mom drank herself to death and my sister overdosed. Hard to believe I'm the sole survivor isn't it?"

Shit, she was far worse off than he was. "That had to be tough."

"Not really. I was a daddy's girl. Mom and my sister were always weak and emotional. I tried to hold them together, but duty called. Mom died while I was overseas the first time. My sister died shortly after I returned the second time. They said it was accidental, but I have my doubts." She gave her strange laugh that he was beginning to understand was more of a self-deprecation. "Ironic when you think about it. I'm the one in a war zone and they're the ones who die. What about you? Do you call home every Friday night like a dutiful son?"

Her tone made it clear she thought the idea pathetic, which irritated him. "No, though I know my parents would love that. We touch base whenever we feel like it. I haven't talked to them in weeks." Something he planned to fix.

"I think once we're out of here, you should call them."

Her voice had softened, and he suddenly understood exactly how alone in the world she was. "Do you ever see your Army—"

"I'm ready to make up my bed and get some sleep. Tomorrow we might break through if we have enough rest." Cooper jumped from his arms even as Riley's boots scraped against the ground. A clear indication she'd stood.

He rose as well, but didn't turn on his phone. It was very low on battery and knowing he probably only had one more time to use his light, he kept it in his pocket. "My phone is about dead."

Without replying, she turned her phone light on and set it on the ground facing up, giving them enough diffused light to see the piles of loose dirt they'd pulled in and the space they had made their home base. She strode to the piles and picking up the gold pan started moving dirt.

He followed suit with the shovel head. It took a while but it wasn't hard work, not like pulling it from the cave-in. After piling more where his head would go, he pulled his handkerchief from his pocket. It was stuck together with Riley's blood. As she knelt by her pile to add her bandana, a shiver raced up his spine. Her bed looked like a newly filled-in grave.

Stuffing his useless handkerchief into his pocket, he caught site of what was left of the towel, Riley had ripped up earlier hanging on the rock. Dog saliva wasn't his pillowcase of choice, but it was better than dirt. He quickly pulled it off and laid it over his constructed pillow.

"I hope you don't snore." Riley pointedly stared at his pillow which was next to her own, though the rail lay between them.

"I don't. Believe it, I'd know. In a firehouse, everyone knows who snores and who doesn't."

She nodded, taking his word for it, as she placed her hat on the ground above where her head would rest.

"Do you?"

Her startled gaze whipped to his. "No, I don't snore, but…"

He cocked his head, waiting.

She shrugged. "I used to talk in my sleep, but not anymore. I'm going to turn the light off as soon as we bed down. You might want to see if you have any rocks to remove." She followed that advice by lying down and settling in. "Not bad."

"No rocks?" He set his hat on a rusted nail in a beam of the old bracing near where they'd worked then returned and lay down.

"Nope. No rocks. You?"

He moved his right leg and pulled out a rock, throwing it toward the pile. Copper ran after it. He laughed. "At least someone likes the rocks."

Riley rolled her eyes, obviously not impressed with Copper's intelligence. "Ready?"

"Ready." The light disappeared and the absolute blackness was back. How long would they sleep? Would their bodies know when it was morning? "Did you happen to see what time it was when you had the light on?"

"It was twenty-one twenty-three."

Nine twenty-three. A good time to sleep after a hard day's work, so why was he wide awake, trying to see in the dark. "You said you've been trapped before. How did you know when to wake up?"

"I set an alarm the first night, but by the next morning I realized what a waste of battery that was. After that I just woke when I woke. I discovered my body was used to sleeping a certain number of hours."

"How many days were you trapped?"

"Eleven."

"Shit. By yourself or were you with others?" She'd avoided the subject while they dug, so he felt no compunction about asking now.

"I thought we were going to sleep?"

"And I thought you were going to tell me about your last experience while we were digging, but you didn't." He'd been well aware that she'd avoided it, but since she'd continued to talk and stay in the present, he'd let it go. But now that she told him she'd been buried alive for eleven days, he had to know more.

Her voice, when it came, was soft. "I was alone. The rest of my comrades had been gunned down before they could escape."

He'd seen people die in fires. Pulled out more bodies than he'd ever wanted to. But he'd never seen someone shot, and

126

certainly never seen someone he knew be killed by bullet or by flame. "That had to be hard to witness."

"I was too busy running for my life to mull it over." There was a tinge of anger in her voice.

"But you must have had too long to think about it later."

At first, she didn't answer, but then a small sigh escaped her, the type he'd seen his sister use when she gave into his niece. "Yeah. The shrink said I had survivor's guilt."

Now that he knew about. They had been fighting the Mongollon Rim fire when one of the teams lost a man. The whole crew were worthless for months. "How did you get away?"

"You're not going to tell me not to feel guilty?"

Her question caught him off guard. "Hell no. I'd feel damn guilty, too."

She must have liked his answer because she continued. "Like I said. I ran. All I had on me was my M9 pistol and M4 carbine. I ran in the only direction that offered any cover. Unfortunately, that meant going up, but the first large boulder I found, I ducked behind and let off a few rounds before continuing to run."

While he didn't know anything about Afghanistan's terrain, he could imagine the scene in the Sonoran Desert. "Did they all follow you or just one?"

She snorted. "Two followed me. The others were busy confiscating our Humvee. That's how they ambushed us. They'd stolen another US Humvee that made us think they were Afghan soldiers, but as soon as I saw them, I yelled. My driver was shot immediately. They grabbed Shaw but Thammishetti and I split up, literally heading for the hills."

She paused, but he hoped she'd continue. She did.

"Tham was shot by the time I made my second cover. I

tried to pick off his pursuers while holding mine at bay, but one of them must have snuck around when my attention was diverted. I heard him yell before it turned into a gurgle. I knew I was on my own then."

"What about Shaw?"

"They tried to use him to flush me out when they lost me. In broken English they yelled that if I gave up, they wouldn't kill him. Before I could make a decision, he told me not to say anything and must have attacked the one holding him because a barrage of bullets went off. I didn't look. That would make his sacrifice worthless."

That he'd understood. "How did you get away." He fervently hoped she escaped capture.

"I found a cave near the top of the mountain and ran inside. It was huge with three tunnels going back into the mountain. I discovered a small hole in one of the walls and once taking off my belt, I was able to squeeze through. It was a small room about the size of the one we found with the old ore car. It was the best I could do with so little time. No sooner had I hunkered down then I heard them in the cave."

He forced himself to uncurl his fingers from the fists he'd instinctually made, but it wasn't easy. Just thinking about her alone, scared, and in danger had his protective instincts spiking. He had to remind himself she was a soldier and trained to survive. She did survive, which was proof of her strength. Still, he itched to protect her even though the story was years ago and far away. "I'm guessing they didn't find you?"

"They came very close, but the man just outside my hole was called back."

He felt the tension leave his body as relief swept through him.

"I listened as they argued near the mouth of the cave. I

couldn't tell what they said, but the tone was pretty clear. They were obviously arguing about what to do with me. They knew I was in there somewhere."

His chest tightened as the decision they made jumped to mind. "They trapped you in."

"Yes." Her voice softened again, the smugness he'd heard earlier at her escape now gone. "They thought I was a serious threat, and they were right, though I didn't know that at the time. Turned out they were on a quiet offensive. I think they couldn't afford to waste time on finding me, so they left. When all was quiet, I shimmied out of my hole and listened. I never trust the enemy to do what I want, and I was right. I don't think it was more than ten minutes before the ground shook and the cave opening, which had stood at least thirty feet high, collapsed."

"What? How?"

"I don't know for certain, but I think they used a grenade launcher and aimed it at the side of the mountain above the cave."

He whistled low. "Were you hit with dirt?"

The odd laugh returned. "No, I was lucky. I was sprayed with dust, but that was it. So that's how I was buried alive the first time. Obviously, I got out."

"But how did you—"

"Nothing personal, Garrett, but I'm tired. Good night."

He clamped down on the myriad questions buzzing through his brain. "Good night." He lay in the inky darkness staring at nothingness, trying to fathom how the woman beside him had managed to get out of a cave with half a mountain between her and the outside world. She had to have been rescued. The Army probably found her dead unit members and followed her trail and blasted her out.

As much as he wanted that to be true, his gut said it wasn't so easy. It didn't take eleven days to find someone's trail and remove enough dirt for a single woman to crawl out, especially with the military's resources.

You don't dig at the bottom. You dig at the top, as high up as you can go. Her words came back to him. *Digging on the bottom will just cause the new earth to fall on top of you.* How did she know that? Did that happen to her? *That would take too much energy. We need to conserve that for digging.* He swallowed hard, his dry mouth gone drier. She'd had to dig her way out of that cave!

He looked in the direction of where Riley lay, her breathing even, letting him know she really had been tired. He tried to go to sleep, but he kept imagining her inside a giant cave of blackness, huddled on the ground, and starving to death.

Luckily, his body finally conquered his mind and he drifted off.

Chapter Nine

Garrett woke. Opening his eyes, he couldn't see a thing. Where were the stars? Were his eyes really open? He blinked twice. They were, but...that's right, he was in the old mine, trapped inside with Riley.

Listening intently, it wasn't hard to hear her breathing next to him. She sounded as if she'd run ten miles, the sounds almost gasping. What the hell? He rolled on his side to wake her when a scratching sounded on her other side.

"Copper?" There was no response but the scratching stopped. He raised his voice a little louder. "Copper? Come here, boy."

Small footsteps approached from behind him. He rolled onto his back and reached out. The dog plopped down beneath his hand, nudging him in the side. "It's okay, boy. We're all here and accounted for."

So, if Copper was on his left, then what was to his right on the other side of Riley? He listened, keeping his arm over the dog, who seemed happy to be with him.

The scratching sounded again then stopped. It sounded like a critter pawed at the wall of the tunnel. There'd been no evidence of any animals living in the tunnel beyond the rabbit Copper had chased in and that made Garrett cautious.

Quietly, he pulled his phone from his pocket, thankful he'd been smart enough to leave a little battery life just in case. Holding it so he hoped it would shine on the animal as soon as he turned it on, he waited for the sound to start again.

After what felt like minutes, the scratching started and he flicked on the light. "Holy shit."

The words burst from his lips without thought. He stared in horror at Riley's bloody fingertips as she dug at the wall in her sleep. Dropping the phone on the ground, he rolled her over to face him. "Riley, wake up."

She moaned in her sleep, her hands reaching out to dig her fingers into his shirt. "Soldier, when I speak to you, I expect you to listen!"

Her eyelids snapped open, and she looked fearful until her gaze rested on him. "What?"

He grasped her to him, keeping her hands between them. "You were dreaming." He held her tight as she struggled to separate, but finally she stilled.

"Dreaming? Did I say anything."

His throat already dry from lack of water suddenly felt scratchy, and he cleared it. "No."

The tension in her body eased. "Good. I've been told when I talk in my sleep, it's not pleasant."

He rested his cheek against her hair, his own heart still pounding as the reality of what she'd endured settled into his soul, leaving him with a strong ache in his chest. He couldn't have let her go at that moment even if the mine was opened large enough for Cyclone to walk in. "You were breathing like you were running a race."

She didn't try to lift her head from his shoulder, instead speaking past him. "Did I wake you?"

He swallowed again. "Yes, but I think you scared Copper."

"Copper?" She turned her head.

Copper sat next to them, watching her as if she'd disappear on him.

She pulled her hand out from between them and reached for the dog, who backed up. "What happened to my..." She pushed away, and he let her go.

She looked back to where she'd been sleeping. Even in the dim light, the brown stains on the grey stone were obvious. "Fuck."

Finding his own equilibrium again, he reached for his light. "I need to clean your hands. Where's your phone?"

She nodded to the small outcropping with the water bottle.

Quickly, he grabbed it up and turned it on, switching his own phone off. Picking up the water bottle, he started to reach for the towel, but it wasn't there. That's right. He used the second half for his pillow. Crap.

Riley stood. "I don't think they're that bad." She held out her hands for him to see.

Not bad? The nails were scraped, and cracked with jagged edges, and she'd rubbed the skin off the tips of her fingers. How long had she been doing that? She must have been pushing hard against the unforgiving rock. His stomach roiled again at the implications. "Is this how you dug your way out of that cave?"

She moved her gaze from her hands to his face. "Yes. There was nothing in there I could use, not even rocks. Just more sand. I used my knife to chip off chunks, but they just fell apart when I tried to use them, and my knife moved less sand than those spikes we used."

"You used your hands."

She shrugged. "It was all I had. I lost every nail, but as you can see, they grew back." Despite her nonchalance, she couldn't hide the shiver as she returned her gaze to her hands.

That had to have been an excruciatingly painful experience. "Well, let's get you cleaned up and assess the damage."

She nodded, still inspecting her hands.

Now he'd have to use his other sleeve for rags, but he couldn't very well ask her to help him rip it off, not with her hands like they were. There was no help for it. Setting the phone against the wall, so the light was angled downward, he unbuttoned his shirt and pulled the knife from his back pocket.

Resisting the urge to turn his back on her, he slipped off his shirt and quickly cut his right sleeve off.

"What happened to you?"

He stilled at her question before continuing his movement to shrug back into the now sleeveless shirt. "Fire."

"That must have been a freaking inferno."

With his right sleeve gone, there was no hiding the scarred mess his arm was. He sighed and finally met her gaze. "It was a wildfire, so yes, I believe that qualifies as an inferno. Now let's get your fingers cleaned up before infection sets in."

She snorted. "Compared to the number of days that they looked worse than this when I was buried alive, I doubt that will happen."

He grabbed up the water bottle, acutely aware that his arm was now exposed. Snatching up the light, he pointed to her "bed." "That may be, but this is a different type of gravel, and I'll not allow you to suffer anymore under my watch. Sit."

"You're watch?" Despite her words, she sat.

He knelt next to her. "You must have heard the term before." He ripped his sleeve length wise and then in quarters. Setting the dirty side down on his thighs, he wet a corner of the first rag.

"Sure, but what makes this *your* watch. Maybe it's my watch."

He immediately dismissed the first justification that came to mind. Telling her it was because he was a male wouldn't fly nor did it sit well with him. He'd always respected women in the fire service and treated them like their male counterparts. He'd been brought up on a ranch run by his mother, yet certain lessons about a cowboy protecting his woman and his home were engraved deep into his psyche. Not that she was his woman, but he definitely felt as if she were in his care. "Let me have your hand. It's my watch because I'm not injured. Not to mention, I'm trained in first aide. Are you?"

"I was years ago, but in this case, I imagine your training is more recent and extensive." He could feel her gaze on him, but didn't dare look to see if she was watching his ministrations to her left hand or staring at his right arm.

"How'd it happen?"

That cleared that up. "Someone decided they had to set off fireworks for the Fourth of July even though there'd been a fire ban in Yavapai County since Memorial Day. The forest went up like a tinder box."

"Duh? I hope your department caught the bastard."

He grinned, even as he carefully removed a pebble from under the skin of her index finger. "That was the easy part. His neighbors were pretty angry since the fire headed for their homes. They lucked-out though. The wind shifted." He took another rag, carefully folding it over her fingers. "Make a soft fist to hold this in place while I work on your other hand."

She did as he instructed then held out her right hand. "Did the wind shift back?"

In hind sight, he wished it had. "No, it moved through Prescott National Forrest northward for days until it threatened a group of homes when it shifted suddenly to the east." He hadn't thought about the fire in detail since his nightmares had stopped, yet he could see everything in his mind as if it were yesterday. Lucky him.

He switched his focus to her hand and wetting another rag, gently cleaned away the dirt. He jerked as he felt the brush of the back of her hand on his right arm.

"Does it hurt?"

He closed his eyes for a moment at the incongruity of the situation. She was the one with fresh wounds, but she took her injuries in stride as if she expected them. Opening his eyes, he finished cleaning her little finger. "No. I'm just not used to anyone touching me. It's not a pretty sight."

Riley moved her gaze from Garrett's arm to his hands where he gently tended to her. There was far more to this firefighting cowboy than she'd realized. She'd been so caught up in trying to keep her inner scars from showing, she hadn't recognized he might have his own scars, and from his reaction, he wasn't happy about them.

She looked at his face, silently urging him to meet her gaze. "When was the last time someone touched your arm?"

He shook his head. "I don't remember. Probably my last physical therapy session."

Physical therapy? For burn scars? She jerked her gaze back to his arm. Were they that bad? The light was diffused and gray, but she could clearly see the bumps and patches that may have been skin grafts. "Was it just your arm?"

He lay another cloth over her left hand. "Make a soft fist."

As she did as he instructed, she waited for him to answer her question. When he rose instead and put what was left of their water back on her rock shelf, it was clear he didn't plan to. "That must have been painful. I had soldiers in my first unit who'd been on the wrong side of an IED. Their pain was excruciating until we could get them to a surgical team. Both times I wished they'd pass out, but they didn't."

She paused as she remembered her first deployment and seeing both men at the base after she was sent home. "When I returned stateside, one had gained a prosthetic leg and a newborn son. The other had lost his hand, and a chunk out of his thigh, but he was doing okay. He was in school training for a new job. Something in cyber security."

Garrett, who was usually the talker, remained eerily uncommunicative. Instead, he returned to his sleeping spot and turned out the light.

Guess they all had their scars to contend with. He'd obviously healed and functioned better than she did. She had to respect that. Laying down, she started to roll on her side to face the wall and froze.

What if morning came and she was digging again? Grasping the soft clothes in her hands, she rolled to her other side to face Garrett. Based on his breathing, he was definitely not asleep. She really should soldier-up, but as she'd learned in bootcamp, her unit was only as strong as the weakest member, and right now that was her. As much as she hated it, she had to ask for help.

"Garrett, can you do me a favor?"

"Yes."

His immediate, unconditional response made her smile. The imp in her wanted to ask for something outrageous like a bowl of apple-cinnamon ice cream or for him to have sex with her. Her humor vanished. And what if he agreed...to the sex part. She hadn't been intimate with anyone in two years. It was tempting, especially with him. Not only was he a good-looking cowboy, but he was a good man, a hero, which made it all that more outrageous. She was anything but.

"What do you need?" His voice in the dark had softened as if he wanted to coax her to trust him.

She already did, implicitly. She hadn't trusted anyone since she left the service. *You haven't gotten close enough to, you idiot. That's because getting close means making a connection.*

Connections to people just ended up causing pain. It was better alone. Yet, she and Garrett needed each other in this particular situation. Her father had always said, *trust your team. Survival is in the team.* Taking a deep breath, she finally spoke. "Will you hold my hand?"

She couldn't quite bring herself to explain why. To admit she'd do more damage to herself was too big a leap. It exposed her weakness too blatantly.

"Of course. I've laid mine on the rail. You find it with your hand. I don't want to do more harm by searching for yours in the dark."

Yup, definitely the hero type. Relieved that he understood or didn't but didn't ask why, she searched out his hand with her own. She found his palm facing up on the rail, it's rough, scarred surface warm against her own palm. She hadn't held anyone's hand for more than a handshake in so long. So long, she didn't remember. But it felt good, plus it had the benefit of keeping her locked facing the rail and not the wall.

When he'd begun to make his "bed" right next to hers, she hadn't been happy, wanting her space, wanting to be alone. Now, she was glad he did. No matter what she wanted, what she needed was to accept that they were a unit until they escaped from the mine. After that, they could simply go their separate ways.

Listening to his breathing, she risked one more question. "Did you happen to see what time it was?"

"Yes, it's just after four. No reason to get up yet." He gave her hand a small squeeze as if to say she needed more sleep.

He was right, she did. Squeezing his hand in silent agreement, she closed her eyes and focused her mind on the last brilliant sunset she'd witnessed, the reds and oranges streaking across the sky as they danced to celebrate the dying day.

~~*~~

"Riley?"

She heard the voice whispering in her ear, but she didn't want to move. Her bed was comfy, and she deserved this, deserved to finally be on vacation and to sleep-in for a change. That's what Caribbean islands were made for.

"Riley, we should get up now."

She snuggled in closer. The man she held was warm and strong and smelled like warm earth after a summer rain shower. "I don't want to."

A chuckle reverberated in the chest beneath her cheek.

"I'm okay with that, but I don't think I can hold off Copper much longer."

Copper? Who was Copper? She didn't have any men in her unit with that last name. Confused, she opened her eyes to ask and found it pitch black. What the hell?

A wet tongue on her right arm had her quickly rolling to the side and sitting up. "Eck."

The man next to her laughed. "I think Copper is going to make for a great alarm clock."

Garrett. The mine. His voice along with the darkness and the dog's wake-up call brought her present reality back in a rush. Shit, had she been sleeping on Garrett? He must think her completely crazy. She ignored the flush in her face and focused on the dog. It was easier. "Glad he won't be waking *me* up."

Obviously clueless to what she'd said, Copper jumped on

her, his target her face. "Seriously, dude?" She kept him away from her face with one hand while she petted him with the other. "I'm happy to see you too, or rather feel you, but you don't see me slobbering all over you."

That brought another laugh from Garrett. "I think he'd be happy if you did."

His voice rose as he spoke, cluing her in to the fact he'd risen. "My guess is Copper is looking for two things."

She stood as much to keep the dog from her as to get up for the day, such as it was. "*My* guess is he wants food and to pee, not necessarily in that order."

The light came on, showing Garrett found the whole situation amusing. Did the man not realize they were still trapped in the mine?

He moved toward her. "How are your hands?"

She held them up, having completely forgotten she'd scraped the hell out of them during the night. "As for manicures, you probably need practice, but my fingers are nicely scabbed."

He took one hand in his and held the light close. "They're okay for now, but you can't dig. You'll rip them open."

"Garrett, I did that every day for eleven days last time and came out alive." She'd been dehydrated, had a fever, and dysentery as well, but he didn't have to know that.

His brows lowered. "This isn't Afghanistan, and you are not alone. You can talk to me while I dig. I doubt there's far to go."

If he thought she would sit on her hands while he did all the work, he was in for a surprise. But first things first. "I think we should all take a trip to the bathroom before we contemplate anything else." She nodded in the direction of the tunnel before glancing at the dirt they had pulled away from the cave-in yesterday. "You've got to be shitting me."

"What?" Garrett turned. "Well, fuck me. We can't catch a damn break." He strode to where the gravel had quietly filled in the area they had cleared, making it look as if they'd done nothing but laze around all day yesterday.

Her heart sank. It was just like back in Afghanistan. She'd half-expected it, but had hoped the different type of soil and the shape of the mountain would be in their favor. So much for hope. "We're still better off than I was overseas, so let's take care of the necessities first," She pointedly looked at Copper who had moved down the tunnel as far the light beam went and stood there looking back at them. "Then we can come up with another plan."

Garrett strolled closer to the dirt pile moving the light so Copper was no longer visible.

Though sure the dog hadn't moved, it still made her uneasy. It made no sense when she'd slept the whole night not knowing where Copper was. Actually, she'd slept soundly once her hands were treated, oblivious to everything, even the fact she'd jumped the rail with her body to lay with Garrett. What did he think about that? Irrationally irritated, she called him. "We can look at that later. Copper has left without us."

At her tone, Garrett swung around. "You're right. Let's go."

He didn't say another word as he led the way. As soon as the light lit on Copper, she relaxed. This time she'd count steps back. She could return without him in the dark and he could have some privacy. At five hundred, he stopped.

"Here you go." He held out her phone. "I'll wait here."

The man was a gentleman through and through. She wanted to say she'd shared a head with men before, but didn't mind not having to. Some of them were pigs. "Thanks." She took the phone and angled it so it revealed the ore cart he had set on the rails the day before. It was about a hundred more steps away. "Come on, Copper."

As if the dog knew his new name, he followed her. When she stepped into the small room, she brought Copper to the far wall. "Okay, you can pee now."

The dog looked at her his tail wagging, his gaze moving from her to the wall.

"Oh, come on. You remember this." She shined the light on the wall until she found where he'd peed the day before. Moving closer to the spot, she pointed, her finger only inches away. "Here. Smell this."

Copper licked her hand before his nose sniffed. Once he caught the sent, he immediately lifted his leg.

She stepped back quickly as he sprayed the wall with a strong steady stream. Shit, the little guy had a big bladder! When he finished, he nosed around and promptly squatted.

She moved out into the tunnel.

"Everything okay?" Garrett called out.

She moved the light to see him. He leaned against the tunnel wall, his arms folded, his feet crossed. In the dark, he looked like the perfect cowboy. "Yeah, just waiting for Copper to finish." She waved her hand in front of her face to indicate the smell.

His chuckle was back.

Inordinately pleased with herself for bringing back his good mood, she swung the light back into the room to find Copper trotting toward her, obviously quite pleased with himself. "You done?"

The dog sat at her feet and pawed at her leg.

Her heart sank. "I don't have anything for you."

Copper pawed again. This is why she didn't own a pet. She sucked at taking care of them. "Go see Garrett." She pointed her hand in Garrett's direction and lit up the area.

Copper's eyebrow rose. He looked at Garrett and back at her.

"Go ahead."

After another double take, the dog finally headed off. She reached into the ore cart and grabbed a carbide can of dirt and brought it back into the room to cover the dog's poop. Returning to the cart, she scooped another can of dirt. For a little dog, he had a large digestive system.

After taking care of her own needs, she headed back to where Garrett waited, Copper sitting beside him. "It's all yours." She handed him the phone. "I'm going to go back and have a mint. I wish I had something to give the dog."

"You can give him one of your mints. You did say they were from a natural store, right?"

She glanced at the dog. "Yes, all-natural ingredients. I guess it couldn't hurt." Feeling better that she could at least offer the dog something, she moved to the left side of the tunnel. She'd laid her finger tips on the wall before realizing that wouldn't work. She'd have no fingertips left if she did that.

"Would this help?" Garrett held out a piece of rotten wood that had fallen off the ore car.

"Definitely. Thanks." She took the wood and held it against the wall of the tunnel and started forward. "Come on, Copper." The light dimmed as Garrett walked in the opposite direction. She was almost at the fork when it finally went completely black. All she had to do was move forward, staying in touch with the wall and being careful how she stepped.

She counted her steps as much to know how close she was to where they had camped as to keep her mind on her surroundings. When she reached five hundred, she stepped across the rail. As her foot sunk in soft dirt, she knew she'd either stepped in Garrett's bed or she'd hit the cave-in.

Crouching, she felt around. When she touched the towel that made his pillow, she grinned. She'd never thought she'd use the skills she developed while trapped in that cave, but they were coming in handy. Carefully, she rose and stepped over to her bed and reached into her back pocket. Taking out a mint, she broke it in half with her teeth. Moving the mints to her front pocket, she sat down. "Okay, Copper. Try this."

The dog jumped on her lap, almost causing her to lose the half a mint. "Whoa, there. I'm not a horse to ride. Here." She held his head and stuck the mint in his mouth. Immediately there was a crunch and then a smacking of his lips. The next second he had jumped off her and barked.

The sound sent loose dirt cascading down the new pile.

"Shh. If you don't like it, I won't give you anymore. Sorry." She sucked on her half. Having Copper with her made her anxious. Knowing he depended on her to survive whittled away at her confidence.

And Garrett? Strangely enough, she wasn't worried about him. He obviously knew a bit about survival and didn't try to pull the macho, "I'm in charge" shit. She respected a man who recognized strength in others.

Her stomach growled, her body reacting to the mint, thinking it was time for breakfast. Hopefully, it would stop before Garrett returned. Working on empty stomachs would make it slow-going for them. She had to figure out how to make her hands useful. There was no way she'd let him do all the work.

It was bad enough she'd slept on the man. It had been far too comfortable, and he was far too nice to look at. For being buried alive, he was the perfect teammate. It had been a long time since she'd been interested in a man, and it hadn't happened once since she'd returned from her second deployment. She just hadn't been around anywhere long enough to get to know anyone.

That was probably why she'd been at Last Chance so long.

All the men were taken and she worked alone most days. It was easy to keep separate. She did have a certain fondness for Annette though. The older woman was what she'd hoped for in a mother, not what she'd had.

She hadn't expected to get to know Garrett either. Then again, what did she really know about him? He could be engaged for all she knew. The thought bothered her. If he was with someone, he shouldn't be letting her sleep on his chest. But if he didn't, he would one day soon. He was the full package. If she wasn't determined to be alone, she'd be interested.

She snorted. Not that he would be interested. He'd already seen what a crazy woman she was. He now knew more about her than half the men she'd served with. Uncomfortable with that thought, she rose. She didn't need to waste time thinking about what Garrett Walker thought of her. What she needed to do is figure out how she could help him dig.

Chapter Ten

Garrett strolled out of the "bathroom" his good mood returned despite the additional dirt he'd have to move. Waking up with Riley sleeping on him, her head nestled in the crook of his shoulder, her arm thrown over his chest, and one of her legs entwined with his had been an unexpected surprise.

Everything about the woman screamed stay away, but in this mine, he'd discovered her softness and her weaknesses, even those she didn't know she had. Her bravery and strength called to him even as her pain and suffering made him want to protect her.

He reached the fork and continued up the rail, his pace quickening with the knowledge he would be with her again. There was something about her that had him wishing more than ever that he wasn't such a scarred mess. He'd pursue her in a heartbeat if he was more 'normal.'

He slowed. Pursue Riley? How exactly would a person do that? He didn't see her as the out-to-dinner and roses kind of woman. More like a night of pool at The Black Mustang, or better yet, a ride into the mountains and camping overnight, making love beneath the stars.

His pace resumed as he grinned. Yes, that's what he would do...if he could. Despite the knowledge that it would never happen, he still enjoyed the daydream. After all, he had her all to himself in the mine where it was pitch black and—He stopped. She wouldn't be able to see him in the dark.

He shook his head and resumed his course. He was an idiot. What she couldn't see, she'd be able to feel, and there was no way he'd make love to her in a dirty old mine, no matter how much he wanted to.

His light finally fell on the end of the tunnel and on Riley's ass as she pulled dirt back from the new pile with the old mining pan. Damn, the woman was going to open her wounds! "Stop! What are you doing?" He ran forward.

She knelt back and dropped the pan. "Bring the light over here."

He stopped next to her. "You're going to open your fingers up again."

She grinned up at him. "No, I'm not. Look." She held her hands up for inspection.

Sure enough, there was no dirt on her fingers. "How?"

"If I hold the pan like this and dig down only halfway, I can move the dirt back as you bring it in. So instead of working side by side, we can work in tandem."

He tried to come up with a reason why it wouldn't work, but that made no sense. He wanted to get out of the mine as much as she did. No, not as much. She needed release far more than he did, and like him, she needed to feel she did her part. He was figuring her out more and more. He nodded. "You're right. That will work."

"Great. Now grab your shovel head and let's get to work. Oh, would you like a mint?"

"Yes, thanks." As she dug in her pocket, he noticed Copper sitting farther away than usual. "Did Copper like his mint?"

"I don't think so. He hasn't come near me since."

Her concern showed in her lowered brow, and he gave her an encouraging smile. "Don't worry. He'll forgive you. They always do."

"And you know this how?" She handed him the roll of mints.

Flicking one out, he put it in his mouth. "I had a dog when I was a boy."

She rolled her eyes. "Of course, you did. I should have known. So, grab your tool and tell me all about him."

"Her." He strode over to where he'd left the shovel head last night, thankful he'd thought to keep their tools by their small camp. If they'd left them where they'd been working, they'd be buried right now.

"Her?" Riley's surprise had him chuckling.

"Yes, her. Her name was Schatzie."

"Odd name for a dog."

Though she spoke about Schatzie, her eyes were on his right arm. He quickly turned the light to focus on their day's work. "She was a unique dog, a German Shepard." He crawled up onto the fresh earth, waited for her to get situated, and quickly turned the phone off, stuffing it in his back pocket. "She was with me from the time I got home from school until I left in the morning."

He pulled dirt through as he spoke. "If I was doing homework, she was laying at my feet." He chuckled, "rather she had a paw on my foot, just to make sure I didn't move without her. She was my best friend for six years."

"Is that a long time?" She scraped dirt farther back.

"You really don't know much about dogs, do you?" He paused in his movements.

"Not a clue. I only know horses. Every other animal under my care has died or run off. It's why I told Whisper she shouldn't leave Copper in my care."

He dug in again. "You'll learn. I did. As it turned out, even I couldn't have known what would happen."

"She got hit by a car."

He stopped again. "No." It was odd how she always went to the worst-case scenario. Then again, maybe it would have been kinder to Schatzie than wasting away. "She had something called EPI or exocrine pancreatic insufficiency. Basically, though she ate, her body wasn't pulling the nutrients from it. Eventually, it shut down. It's a very unusual problem and is difficult to diagnose. By time we figured it out, it was too late."

"You must have missed her." More dirt rolled over the edge as she pulled it back. "Did you get another dog then?"

His parents had talked about it, but.... "No."

"Why not?"

"It's hard to explain. I loved that dog. Losing her left a hole in my heart. Of course, with time I moved on. I just didn't want to love another dog only to lose it. That happens with dogs. Different breeds live longer. German Shepherds usually live to be about twelve or more. Smaller dogs like Copper can live longer. But either way, they don't live as long as us. I didn't want to experience that pain again." She probably thought him a wimp of a man for that. He tried to think of a defense, but he couldn't.

She didn't say anything for a long time. Not only did that concern him, but it also hindered his efforts to dig straight. "Hey, you still there? You're not crying over my dog story, are you?"

"No, I was thinking about the people I've lost. I totally get where you're coming from. It's better not to get that close again."

People? Probably because of her family. Someday though, she'd have her own family. He tried picturing Riley with a baby. He couldn't do it. Instead, he saw her with a teenage boy, teaching him how to shoot at a target range. He grinned. Now that fit her perfectly. "Tell me about these pets of yours."

As she spoke, he kept digging, half of his mind on her story and the other half on getting her out of the mine safely.

The day was spent digging and talking. He told her more about growing up with an older sister who thought she was his third parent and a younger brother who liked to compete with him. She spoke mostly about her time in the Army, though she did share a story about a prom date gone bad and having to be picked up at the police station for underage drinking.

He learned more about her by what she didn't talk about than by what she did. She didn't talk about her family except an occasional word about her father. She never spoke about her pets, though he now understood why she knew so much about horses. "Your parents didn't mind you living in the stables?"

"They didn't know. As far I was concerned, at the ripe age of fifteen, I didn't need them anymore. Turned out, I didn't, which was a good thing."

He pulled more dirt to the side before responding. Having her right behind him helped even more with his direction. The gravel seemed more condensed. He wasn't sure what that meant, but it felt like he was making better progress. "Why was that good?" Though he'd left home at the usual age and begun his own life, he was glad to have both his parents still living.

She let out her self-deprecating chuckle. "Because when I turned seventeen, my father went overseas and my mom was a basket case, so she depended on me instead of the other way around. She was weak."

The last was said with so much derision that he felt the need to defend the woman. "In what way was she weak? I'm sure being an Air Force wife isn't easy, especially with two daughters."

Riley pulled dirt, the gravel rolling back before she answered. "She was nothing but emotion. Couldn't get her to see the logic in anything. It was all about how *she* felt. It was frustrating and a waste of breath to try to talk sense into her. If she wanted something a certain way or an item in the store, that was what had to happen, even if it made no sense." The movement of dirt behind him stopped.

He pulled more toward him with the shovel head and pushed it to the left of him. When he didn't hear her gold pan, he paused. Had she gone back into the past again? "Riley?"

"Yeah, I'm still here. Just thinking."

"About your mother?"

"No, Big Bird. Yes, about my mother. She and my father were complete opposites. He was logical, stoic, rational, and strong. She was emotional, always ridiculously happy or incredibly depressed. I have no idea why they ever got married."

"Opposites attract?"

She snorted. "Or maybe my father couldn't help but fall for a woman who needed him. Whatever the reason, they should have never been man and wife." Her gold pan hit the dirt again.

Relieved that she simply reminisced, he chuckled. "But if they hadn't married, you wouldn't be here." He dug the shovel head deep ahead of him.

"You're kidding right. If they hadn't married, I wouldn't be in this godforsaken mine? Sounds like a win to me."

He recognized her humor now. "True, maybe you'd be on an island sipping pina coladas."

"Presidente."

He pulled the earth toward him. It was definitely heavier and it seemed colder, which made no sense. "What president?"

"No, the beer. It's what I drink when I'm in the Caribbean."

This was new. "And how often have you been there?" She hadn't mentioned being stationed there.

"Not enough. Just a few times. You should go. It makes for a perfect vacation."

He had never had the urge to go to the Caribbean. The people he knew either went north to the mountains in the summer or to Rocky Point, Mexico in the winter for vacation.

"Hey, is this dirt getting heavier or am I just getting weaker from a lack of food?"

Though her question was said half in jest, it confirmed what he'd been thinking. "I noticed that, too. Let's take a look." He brushed his hands off on his jeans and pulled out the phone. Half-covering it with his hand, he turned on the light. "What the hell?"

"What?" She crawled forward, squeezing in next to him.

"It looks wet. Hold this." Handing her the light, he picked up a clump with his hand. "It *is* wet." He brought it close and sniffed. "Rain."

"Rain? As in outside? As in it rained outside and we are near to breaking through?" She pushed past him, crawling forward a foot, the excitement in her voice concerning him.

They hadn't even dug as far as they had the day before. How could they be close to the outside of the mine? "I don't think that's it."

"What else could it be?" She put her palm to the end of the hole he'd been digging. "I don't feel any air." She examined the darker earth with the light, following its color where it met the dry dirt. "It can't be an underground spring. This is coming from above."

"Monsoon." Fuck. They really couldn't catch a break.

She looked back at him. "What do you mean monsoon? That while we were in here last night, a monsoon came through?" Her tone had risen, her deeper almost raspy voice sounding more like an eight-year-old girl now.

Shit, he needed to keep her calm. "Yes, I think that's what happened. That could be good. It may have washed a lot of loose dirt away."

Her widening eyes suddenly narrowed. "Or it could have caused a mud slide and buried us deeper."

Her anger made it clear she didn't like being coddled. Fine, that was exactly what probably happened. "It may have, but it also would make the dirt more stable."

She crawled backward, shaking her head until she'd left the pile of dirt they'd been working on and stood on the tunnel floor. "I'm not staying in here for another eleven days."

Shit, this wasn't good.

He scrambled backward, his gaze riveted to her shaking head. "You won't have to. We'll be out of here in two days or less. I'm sure Wyatt has already called Cole and he's returned to start searching for us."

"Don't you see? They won't find us. Domino would know enough to go home with a monsoon coming. You said survival would overcome training. With the monsoon, any tracks we left are gone, and if she went back to the ranch, there's no way for them to know where we are."

Her voice was rising in volume now as well. He had to keep her calm. "They don't have tracks, but they do know they have two loose horses with saddles which means we are in the area somewhere. How many places can there be to look? From what I saw, except for the hill Cole's house sits on, this valley is flat and easily reviewed. That leaves the surrounding mountains and this mine."

Her shaking head had slowed. "But that could take days."

Slowly, he slid off the pile and stood. He could feel how

much she wanted to hope. He had to find something for her to cling to. "Didn't you say Cole was supposed to take Cyclone and pull the loose beams at the entrance to this mine back to his house?"

Her head stopped. "Yes, so?"

He relaxed. "So, that means he knows the mine isn't safe and what the mine looked like just days ago. All he has to do is check this place, see the cave-in and know we're here."

She remained silent, her mind obviously processing what he said. When her head started to shake again, he tensed. "With the mudslide, he won't know we were trapped in here before that occurred. Or he might think we were buried alive under it. We're never fucking getting out of here!"

Even as she threw the phone to the ground, light snapped across the tunnel like lightning and he leapt across the space between them. He grabbed her by the shoulders. "Riley, listen to me. We *are* getting out of here."

"No! No. No. No, no."

His chest tightened at the hopelessness in her voice, and he pressed her to him, holding her tight, despite her struggles to get away. "Shh, I promise, we will get out of here. I won't stop until we're free. It's okay. You're not alone."

She stopped struggling and the tension left her, but he didn't let her go. Instead, he held her, soothing her, putting his conviction into his words, silently willing her to hang on.

"I can't."

Her mumbled words, had him loosening his hold.

She pulled her head from his shoulder. "I can't. I can't do this."

He looked into what he knew were dark brown eyes, despite their black appearance, and a chill raced through his heart.

Lifeless.

It was as if the mine had sucked all of her psyche into its depths and left a soulless shell.

Desperate to save her, he angled his head and kissed her.

Her unresponsiveness didn't deter him. He *had* to reach her. Pulling her closer, he breached her lips, teasing her tongue, coaxing her to feel. She stood in his embrace, limp, with no reaction at all. Moving his hand into her hair, he ran his fingertips against her scalp, slanting her head to better taste her.

His heart pounded in his chest as if he were in the middle of a burning forest, using every ounce of energy to battle the flames. But he had no flames to battle here. He had to stoke the flames. Instinctually, he moved his other hand to cup her ass and squeezed.

Her mouth opened wider, and he wrestled her tongue with his own before squeezing her again.

A cry low in her throat sounded like part despair and part passion just before she thrust her tongue into his mouth.

Relief, triumph, and excitement filled him as her arms wrapped around his neck and she pressed closer to him, as if she could climb inside him. There was no shyness in her actions as she ground her hips against his growing erection, and her tongue explored his mouth. Her passion was like her, straightforward and strong.

He ran his hand down her back to the edge of her tank top. His finger buried under it and moved up her side, under the stretch bra, until he touched the softness of her breast.

Her moan filled his mouth as she turned her body to give him better access.

The invitation too enticing to ignore, he moved his fingers over the round plumpness until he brushed across her hard nipple. Raw desire tightened his balls, reminding him how long it had been since he was with a woman. But Riley was no ordinary woman, and a glimmer of hope started deep in his chest.

Suddenly, her hand cupped his cock.

He grabbed her wrist and tried to pull away, but she wouldn't let his mouth go. Finally, he had both her hands in his and stepped back.

"What's wrong?" Her brows lowered in confusion. "I want you."

His cock jumped at her words. His own insecurity and his conscience combined to give him some control. "I don't want to take advantage of our—"

"Don't go all cowboy on me. I need that smoking hot firefighter right now." Her gaze slipped from his and the haunted look came back. "I don't believe in tomorrow anymore." She closed the distance, her gaze focused on his and yet not. Her voice lowered to a whisper. "I need to feel alive."

He couldn't refuse if he wanted to, and he didn't want to. He wanted to give her everything she needed and more. He closed the distance between them and cupped her face in his hands. "You are alive. You're a beautiful strong woman with a fire of survival inside."

Her gaze switched from one of his eyes to the other. "Make me feel it, Garrett."

She didn't say please, but her eyes begged him.

He lowered his head to gently brush her lips with his own, let her know he cared, then he gave her what she wanted.

Riley's heart skipped a beat at the same time excitement rushed to her core as Garrett backed her against the wall and devoured her mouth, his scruffy chin a reminder that he was all male and then some. She closed her eyes and let the feelings flow through her. *Yes! I want this! No, not this —him.*

His hands pushed up her tank even as his legs leaned into her, keeping her pinned. As he stroked both her breasts, his tongue swept through her mouth like a forward scout team, leaving no spot unexplored.

When his thumbs and forefingers lightly squeezed her nipples, she arched, wanting more. He didn't disappoint, alternately squeezing and pinching both, causing her sheath to moisten with desire.

His hand left her right breast, and she moaned in disappointment, opening her eyes to see him looking down. At his touch on her stomach, she sucked in a breath. He understood it for the invitation it was and made short work of unbuttoning and unzipping her jeans.

His hand slipped beneath the elastic of her panties but stopped when he found her watching him. He gazed into her eyes for what seemed like forever before his hand continued downward and his finger found her clit.

The spike of excitement shot right to her core, and she wanted to close her eyes and enjoy, but his gaze held hers as if daring her to look away. She'd never backed down from a dare. She grasped his muscular shoulders and didn't blink.

As if he knew she accepted his silent challenge, his lips moved into a slow small smile just before two of his fingers made tiny gentle circles over her clit. Staring into his eyes as he brought her body to the edge of orgasm had to be the most erotic experience she'd ever had. Her own stubbornness helped, her whole body tingling with heat and need.

A slight shift in his eyes was the only warning she had before his finger moved swiftly between her folds and sunk deep inside her sheath. The feelings sent her to her toes and she caught her breath, but kept her gaze pinned to his.

He raised his eyebrows slightly as if he took her stubbornness as a challenge. Just the thought had her squeezing his fingers inside her. He lost his smile at her movement and a short surge of triumph whistled through her before his thumb found her clit and lazily played with it.

Though she kept her eyes on his, her body continued to tighten as the exquisite shards of pleasure spiked through her until her body betrayed her. Her orgasm swept through like a dust storm. She had no use for traitors, but as her eyes closed, she gloried in the uplift of satisfaction in his expression that both pleased and overwhelmed her.

When she opened her eyes, she found her hands holding tightly to Garrett's shoulders, her rock among the chaos of feeling. He didn't smile, but the knowing in his eyes had her imp coming out of hiding.

Without thought, she moved her hand to his belt buckle.

He grabbed her wrist. "Don't. You'll rip open your scabs."

She blinked, having completely forgotten about her hands and the damage she'd done them. "Then you do it."

He didn't shake his head, but she could read the denial in his body language. When had she begun to know him so well? "If you don't, I will. My fingers be damned. I want to feel you inside me. Make me feel you."

His nostrils flared. He gazed at her as if to determine if she really meant it.

She did.

Finally, he unbuttoned his jeans.

She pushed her own jeans off her hips, but didn't get far before his cock rubbed against her mons. She snapped her head up.

His eyes were focused on her own, and despite the limitations of her jeans, she bent her legs, and he pushed his cock between her folds to her entrance. There was no smile on his face now, just steady concentration. Was he going slow on her account?

She stared into his eyes. "Now."

Despite her command, he slowly slid inside her until he was fully sheathed.

She closed her eyes and leaned her head back against the rock, the feeling of him inside her filled every need she had and some she didn't know she had.

His hands bracing against the rock on either side of her had her opening her eyes again. He leaned his forehead against hers as he slowly pulled back his hips. "Only for you."

She wasn't sure if it was his words or his body as he thrust into her, but every part of her melted as he started the buildup that would satisfy them both this time.

As a lover, he was everything he promised to be, bringing her with him, holding his own release until she began and then prolonging her pleasure as he joined her. When they both were done, she had her head on his shoulder as he held her against him, their bodies still one.

He lowered his head to speak in her ear. "Do you feel alive now?"

She grinned and nodded against his shoulder.

A soft chuckle vibrated in his chest. "Me too."

She should probably move away and pull herself together, but really, what was the rush?

Garrett's stomach rumbled.

Ah, and there was the rush. She lifted her head. "Do you want another mint?"

"No, it will go away. But we need to turn off your phone light or we won't have it when we need it."

She pushed back from him, though he kept them anchored at the hip. "Shit. We need to do that now." She looked over his shoulder to see her phone sitting on its side, facing the other wall. In front of it was Copper, watching her.

It was an odd sensation. "I'm not sure Copper approved of us having sex when we should be working."

Garrett shrugged. "Good thing he's not our captain then." His smile was wide, but as he separated them, irritation flashed through her. Why did survival always have to get in the way of actually living?

Quickly, he scooped up the phone and turned it off.

In the pitch blackness, she pulled up her jeans and straightened her tank. "So now what?"

He moved next to her. "I suggest we sit down and re-evaluate our plan."

She was all for that. Her knees felt like rubber at the moment. Sitting down right where she stood, she leaned her back against the wall. "Copper. Come here boy."

The sound of the dog's feet stepping on the gravel relieved her, but when he tried to climb in her lap and lick her, she was back on guard again. "Really, Copper?"

Garrett took a seat next to her. Very close, in fact. Told you he'd forgive you."

"True, but it doesn't really matter if I can't keep him alive long enough to return him to Whisper."

He chuckled. "That's if he wants to go back to Whisper."

She finally wrestled Copper onto her lap with his head facing away from her. "He won't have a choice. I can't keep him."

"Why not?"

At the surprise in Garrett's voice, she turned her head to face him. "Because I move around too much. It would limit the ranches I can work at. I'm sure some have their own dogs."

"Then don't move around. Stay here at Last Chance."

That sounded far more tempting than it should, but it wouldn't be good for her or anyone else. Hadn't he noticed what a mess she was? He'd certainly seen and learned more about her overseas adventures than anyone else. Even more than her Army shrink before her discharge.

Sure, she received an "honorable" discharge, but the shrink had basically said she wasn't fit to return to service. What the hell did he know? She was lucky she had ranch hand experience to fall back on. She'd heard of other service people being completely lost when returning to civilian life and blowing their brains out. She didn't mention *that* to Garrett. One member of her unit from her first tour had gone back three more times, surviving intact until he came home. His funeral was the last time she'd seen anyone from the Army.

"I know Cole would appreciate you staying here. If I were you, I'd ask for hazard pay after all this." Garrett's voice brought her back to the present.

It was better to focus on the present, not the past or the future. "Do you really think the wet dirt will hold up better? Because if it will, we should try digging a smaller tunnel through it. It would get us out of here faster. Plus, we wouldn't want it to dry or it might cave in on us again."

He took her change of topic in stride. "I do. We can go back to a two foot by two foot and see how far we can get. How are your hands holding up?"

She touched the tops of her fingers. Her nails were sharp enough to cut something, but her fingertips were just a little sore. "They're fine." She checked the wrap on her arm. "But your sleeve on my arm is a little loose." She wasn't about to tell him that it stung quite a bit. There wasn't anything he could do about it, and he'd try to keep her from working.

"I'll fix it when we start working again."

That worked for her. "No time like the present."

"No, let's wait a bit. I think Copper needs some attention. We've ignored him for most of the day."

Was he recovering from the sex they had? Hmm, that could be it. She could wait. She just hoped it wouldn't be too long. She'd already proven that the longer she was in the mine, the more she slipped into craziness.

Chapter Eleven

"Coming out." Garrett backed out of the narrow tunnel he'd been digging. Riley's removal of the dirt behind him made it easy to do. It was a bit tight, but they didn't need a highway to get out of there.

"Calling it quits for the night?" Riley's voice sounded relieved.

He should have quit earlier. She never complained, so it was easy to forget she was wounded. She may not say anything, but he could tell her injuries were sapping her strength. It didn't help that they had no food. "Yes. I'm ready for roasted rabbit. Do you think we could get Copper to run for take-out?"

"Only if you tip him with a nice juicy steak." He could almost see her smirking.

After a day of talking, he could tell exactly what mood she was in and even more importantly when she was slipping into the past again. He'd been told that people who'd experienced trauma should talk about it to "process" it. They made him do that while he was in the hospital.

But with Riley, every time her last cave-in came up, she started to go back to that time. It might be because this was far too similar. She'd slipped back only twice all day.

She turned the light on, and he slid down from the moist pile of dirt.

"What I wouldn't do for a big snake right now."

At her words, he stilled. She'd talked about eating a snake, a bird, and beetles in her last experience. He didn't want her to slip back again. "I think we should change it up. Let's chew on my gum tonight."

"That will make us hungry."

"Yes, but we'll be asleep when we're hungry so we can look forward to a mint in the morning."

She put her hand on her hip. "Well, you certainly know how to wine and dine a woman."

He smirked at her. Oh, he knew how to do that, but it didn't help in the end. So where did that put him with Riley? He'd tried not to, but he'd be fooling himself if he said he didn't have feelings for her. And he'd been doing so well to avoid getting his heart broken again. He was an idiot.

"I'm taking Copper down to the bathroom. We'll be back in a bit."

"Don't forget your stick." He pointed to the piece of wood she used to follow the cave walls in the dark to their bathroom. She'd used it a couple times during the day. There was something normal about it now that bothered him.

"I wouldn't leave without it." Obviously, in a good mood, she called the dog and moved to the right wall. Getting into position, she turned the light out and started down the tunnel, talking to Copper as if he understood every word.

Feeling his way to their camp, he sat on his bed and pulled out his gum. He only had a couple sticks. It wouldn't be long before working in the dirt all day would be impossible without nourishment. Though he kept a positive view, he was worried. He didn't actually have faith in Cole finding them in time.

She'd made it eleven days last time, but she had food. While they could last a number of days, digging would be out of the question. They had very little water left in the single water bottle and the only chance of finding water was if they went down a shaft. His concern was whether they could get back up.

He had no choice but to dig tomorrow until they reached fresh air. It was the only plan that had a chance of success. They'd both have more staying power if he hadn't given into her plea for sex. It went against his grain to make love to her in the dirt, but he didn't regret it. He had brought her back with his kiss and had enjoyed every moment of being with her.

Now that they'd been together, would she sleep with him tonight? He hoped so. It had been an unexpected pleasure finding her laying on him when he woke. Though he knew he was torturing himself with the normalcy of it, he still wanted it while he could have it. Once they left the mine...

Her voice far back in the tunnel had him anticipating her entrance. She had no clue that she'd be keeping Copper. If the Whisper woman was even half what Riley said she was, she'd make Riley keep the dog. At least he'd know she had a good companion.

He could make out her words now.

"Just wait until we're out of here. I'm sure Annette will have something in the house for you to eat. Just don't eat too much. That won't be good for you. Maybe you should play with a rock or something to keep your mind off eating."

He waited until she was closer then spoke. "Did Copper do well?"

"He did. I think he's tired. That's a long walk for him." As she drew close to him, she turned on the light, facing it away from them. "Here you go."

He took it and stood. "Here." He handed her a stick of gum.

She promptly unwrapped it and put it in her mouth. She had a beautiful mouth with full lips that he loved kissing. Shit, now who was losing it. "Be back." Turning out the light, he headed for the small bathroom, his fingers on the wall guiding him. Her idea to designate it as such, along with the towel pieces and ore cart of dirt just proved how much she had gone through by herself.

The thought of her alone for eleven days buried alive had his stomach turning in on itself. At least he was with her this time. Though she regressed back in time on occasion, her strength in functioning at all had him in awe. He wasn't so sure he could handle it if something like this happened to him again.

Arriving at the bathroom, he used it quickly then headed back. He didn't like leaving her alone too long. As he drew closer, he heard scraping. His heart thudded in his chest that she was scraping the wall again. Turning the light one so he could run to her, he instead found her emptying her gold pan of dirt onto his "bed."

She looked up. "You're wasting light."

She was right, so he ran up to save time. "What are you doing?"

"I'm adding my dirt to yours. This way you can have a bigger bed, and I can sleep on you." She stared at her handiwork, but when he didn't respond she looked at him uncertainly. "If that works for you."

Worked for him? It worked way too well. He tamped down his pleasure. "That makes sense." He moved to where she'd built up the bed but still left the rails showing. She probably didn't want to roll past them. She stood to the side as he lay down then joined him after turning the light out and putting it in her back pocket. Copper, not to be far from her, lay at their feet.

The added dirt was somewhat comfortable, but with her

lying next to him, it wouldn't have matter. It felt so right, he had no doubt he'd sleep well.

Her hand lay on his chest, her head on his shoulder, his bare right arm behind her. It was the perfect setup.

"Thanks. I feel safer this way."

Surprised she'd admit it, his chest warmed. He wanted to say he'd always keep her safe, but that wasn't his place. "I'm glad I can help."

Before he realized what she had done, the top button of his shirt was undone. He grabbed her hand. "What are you doing? You're going to hurt your fingers."

"No, I'm not. Your buttonholes are plenty big. And don't worry, I used a rock to grind down the sharp edges of my nails. They were driving me crazy."

He wasn't worried about her nails.

"Are you going to let my hand go now?"

All his feelings of contentment disappeared. "Why did you unbutton my shirt?"

The smile was back in her voice. "So I can lay my hand on your chest. Why else?"

"I don't think that's a good idea."

He felt her shift so she had to be looking at him though she couldn't see him. "What are you afraid of? I've already seen your scars. They don't bother me."

No, what she'd seen was the least of it. What she hadn't seen was what had scared off every woman he had thought might like him enough to ignore them. He was wrong. No one could ignore them. "They're not something you need to subject yourself to."

"Wait, I can have sex with you but can't touch you?"

He grimaced. It did sound odd when she put it that way. "Are you sure?"

"Listen, you've seen most of my scars. In fact, you've seen more of them than anyone else including the Army shrink. I think I can handle yours in the dark."

It had been two years since a woman looked at his scars and couldn't hide her revulsion. At least in the dark, he wouldn't have to see Riley's expression, but he would know by the tone of her voice exactly what she thought.

"Well?"

He had no decent excuse to give. "Fine, but let me unbutton my shirt so you don't hurt yourself."

"Thank you."

Reluctantly, he unbuttoned the next three buttons. "Okay, you can lie down now."

She laid her head back on his shoulder and with unerring accuracy, slipped her hand inside his shirt. At first, she moved it to his left side which was mostly normal, but as she moved it closer to herself, he tensed.

"Will you relax? It's not like I'm going to scratch you. I told you, I scraped my nails down."

Realizing she'd done that for him, he tried to breathe normally.

Her hand moved across the major burn scars on his right side. Not once did she stop the movement, trailing her palm across his ragged skin before coming to rest over his heart. "There, that wasn't so terrible was it?"

Her words surprised him. "No."

"So how did you get so badly burned? You said it was a wildfire, but many of you Hot Shots fight them and don't get burned. Why you?"

"Because I lost sight of what was important." The bitter words came out of their own accord. He hadn't told anyone that was how he felt, but here in the dark with a woman he could have spent the rest of his life with if not for his rash act, they just spilled out.

"You said life was more important than structures."

"It is. And no lives were in jeopardy...of the fire. I should have just pulled back when it got dangerous."

"But you didn't."

He shook his head even if she couldn't see him. "No, I didn't. We were building a fire break between the forest and a small cluster of ramshackle homes. I just needed to get one more tree down, so I told my crew to pull back while I finished that final tree. I never saw the burning pine falling toward me until it was too late. I heard a shout and looked up. I held my arm up to cover my face and turned away just before I was knocked over."

"Oh, God. That must have been excruciating."

"Not at first. When I fell, I hit my head on a stump and lost consciousness. When I woke up in the hospital, I hurt, but had no idea how bad the damage was with all the pain medication I was on. It wasn't until my family came to see me after the doctor got me stable that the pain seeped through. I had third degree burns on almost half my body."

"That was only the beginning though, right. I've known soldiers who were badly burned from grenades and IEDs. There's skin grafts and surgeries and stuff."

"Yes, and stuff."

"How many weeks before they were done fixing you?"

"They had to do multiple grafts at different times. It took five months."

"Shit." She remained quiet and for that he was thankful. Just remembering the pain of the burns had his stomach rolling.

"Tell me. You don't seem like a cocky man who makes rash decisions. Why did you stay to get that last tree down if no one's life was in danger?"

"I guess you could say it was an emotional decision instead of one of the logical ones we're all trained in. As we reached the staging site, I was waiting for the update when the people who lived in the small cluster of homes drove slowly by. Some of the vehicles looked like they wouldn't make it to the next town. In one of them was a little girl with a blue stuffed animal. She looked at me, her eyes wide with fear as she sat on her mom's lap. Her mother held her, tears streaming down her face." It still amazed him how clear their images still were.

"They were sorry to leave their homes, but they must have been relieved to get out in time."

Riley's observation was the same he had. "That's what I thought, until I saw the homes. These weren't nice log cabins or fancy adobe homes. Once we got our orders, we drove by the small community of shacks. I have no other word for it. I understood then why the mother was in tears. Those shacks were all they had. The only thing standing between them and living on the street."

Riley shifted again and her voice came from slight above him. "You wanted to save their homes."

He nodded before remembering she couldn't see him. "Yes. I was determined, and only one tree stood between myself and my goal, but I knew it was dangerous. It was why I sent my men back. I'm just glad the only person's life I endangered was my own. The only person's life I ruined was mine." It had been a stupid decision, and he'd paid the price. He'd been trained better and didn't deserve to be a firefighter, never mind a Hot Shot.

"Did it work?" Her voice was soft. "Were the homes saved?"

"I don't know. I never asked. I never went back. They had the fire eighty percent contained when I woke up, but I was in my own hell. It didn't matter anymore."

"I'm sure it did to those families. What if they were able to go home because of what you did?"

He'd thought about that over the last few years. "And what if they didn't? I would have ruined my life for nothing. I'd rather not know."

"You keep saying you ruined your life." Her voice was normal now. "You don't seem ruined."

He blinked. He lived with it for so long, he thought it was obvious to everyone. "You felt my chest. My leg, my ass, even my foot are nothing but a mess of scar tissue and skin grafts. Most of those coming from my inner thighs and back. No one wants to live with someone who looks like me."

Riley snorted. "Seriously? You need a reality check. I can name seven men right off the top of my head that came home looking a lot worse than you do. Their wives were just happy they were alive."

"And what about the ones who had no wives to come home to? Have they met someone who can live with who they are now?"

To her credit, she didn't answer right away. "I know three like that. Last time I saw them, one was engaged, one had a girlfriend and the third was still very single."

"I guess I'm in the final third then."

Her hand moved over his chest again, making him tense. "Have you actually ever let a woman see these scars?"

He swallowed. "Two women have. It was too much for them."

Riley swore. "Bitches."

His hand caught hers on his chest. "No, they weren't. They were good women. They couldn't help their reaction. No woman should have to look at this every morning."

171

"Bullshit." Her anger was burning so hot, she couldn't seem to find any real words. Furious with the prisses who couldn't see the heroic man beneath the scars, she pulled her phone from her pocket and turned the light on before he could react.

"Stop."

"No." She moved her hand out from under his and sat up, pulling the right side of his shirt with her.

He grabbed her hand with the phone, his own large one shutting out the light. "Don't. You don't need to see it."

She jerked her hand out of his and shined the light on his chest. She let her eyes roam over every inch of patchworked skin. Was it pretty? No. He was right, it was a mess of scars and bumps. The skin wasn't all the same skin tone either. It had to have hurt like the devil. He was lucky he hadn't gone crazy from the pain.

Was his chest horrific? No. When she'd seen her fill, she angled the light to the ceiling. "So what? You have some scars. I've seen far worse. Hell, there are those of us whose scars don't even show, but we are far more messed up than you. At least you lived."

He had turned his head away from the light, but now he faced her. "Are you going to try to tell me it's a pleasant sight?"

It was the first time she'd heard sarcasm from him. Though it surprised her, she understood where it came from. He had his limits, and she'd pushed him beyond. But as far as she was concerned, it was for his own good. "Hell no. It's ugly. But some people are born ugly and have no brave tale to tell. You were lucky."

"Right, fucking lucky."

If she could have crossed her arms and held the light, she would have. "You are. Only half your body was burned. Most of it you can cover up to hide it if you want to, though I'd dress for comfort and screw everyone else and what they thought. Plus, your face is unmarred. I know a man who only has one eye and half a nose. Hair won't grow on half his head so he shaves it every day. You're a handsome man and people don't turn away from you in the grocery store."

"You think I'm handsome?"

She rolled her eyes. "That's what you decide to listen to?"

He shrugged. "It's not like I could tell. We've been in the dark most of the time. And by the way, I think you're beautiful."

"You need your eyes checked." She turned the light off and stuffed it back in her pocket.

"Come here." His voice had a smile in it.

She liked that she could make him smile. What was with that? Still, she willingly lay back down and ran her hand over his chest. "If a woman really cared about you, she wouldn't let you get away just because of this. You just haven't found the right woman."

"Or maybe I have, and she just doesn't know it yet."

His voice was soft, but still it sent a shiver through her. She was no good at caring for people. In fact, she sucked at it as her mom often told her, but it took war for her to finally get it through her thick head. "I think you're delirious from lack of food. You better go to sleep."

He gave her a little squeeze. "Yes, Ma'am."

She shook her head against his chest. He was a good man. The kind she respected, which just made it more dangerous for her to be around him. She should be sleeping in a completely different tunnel if she were smart, but there was no way she was leaving his side. He made her feel safe. He respected her in turn, and he gave her hope. Right now, that was the only thing keeping her alive.

Plus, he'd made her body feel better than it had in years.

Closing her eyes, she smiled. Hopefully, her dreams would be filled with him. After all, they were only dreams.

The next morning, she woke refreshed. Not a single bad dream entered her mind. She was going to start thinking of Garrett as her nightmare blocker.

After their usual routine, though it was depressing that they had one, they grabbed their tools and moved back to the cave-in. Garrett had mentioned checking her arm, but she'd distracted him. There was no doubt in her mind it was infected. She had ibuprofen, but only one dose. She planned to take it when the pain got too bad. Right now, it was just hot and it stung a bit.

He moved the light to shine on their progress from the day before. With the dense dirt, he had moved forward at least twelve feet. She wasn't sure, but she estimated the cave-in had happened fifteen feet inside. The problem was that the mudslide could have changed everything.

Garrett climbed up on the mound of dirt. She looked for Copper and found him lying on the earth where they had slept. After giving him a little water and forgoing her own, he'd settled there. He wasn't doing well. He had a lot less fat on his bones and the lack of food was making him weak.

She voiced her fear. "I don't think Copper can hold out many more days."

Garrett looked over her shoulder at the dog. "No, he can't. We better start digging then."

Climbing up behind him with her gold pan, she set her position directly behind him.

When he saw she was ready, he faced forward, dug his shovel in, and turned out the light. There wasn't much battery life left on her phone now either. In her cave, there had been little tufts of straw paper packing material from the boxes of guns and ammunition that had been stored there. She lit those when her phone had died.

If they were forced to, they could bring wood up from the transfer area they'd found, but she wasn't excited about burning up oxygen.

At first, they worked in silence, but she knew she had to talk to keep him pointed in the right direction. "Why did you buy a house here if all your family live in Prescott?"

He pushed a shovel full of dirt behind him to his left. She leaned forward and dragged it all the way out to send it down the small hill they had made. The movements became automatic. Their tunnel had to be at least twenty feet now. Getting the dirt out took longer.

"I needed a change of scenery and since I'd worked at the Canterbury fire station for a couple of years, I figured this area was as good a spot as any. Close to family but not too close."

That made sense. He wanted to stay away from his smothering sister. "Will you join that station again?"

He didn't respond right away and when he did it was so quiet, she almost missed it. "No."

Knowing how he felt about getting burned on the job, she dropped it. "Is the station around here a good one?"

As she expected, he launched into a description of the men he'd served with. Most of his stories were funny as it seemed they liked to play pranks on each other. But some were poignant about the people they'd saved.

Suddenly, he stopped working, and more importantly he'd stopped talking.

She leaned forward into the tunnel he'd created. "Everything okay up there?"

"Shh."

She froze. Did he hear something? Was it people outside? A hawk? Water? She wanted it to be people. She'd never heard what it would be like to have people rescue her. The anticipation and hope were almost too much.

"We're here! In here!" Garrett's yell sounded loud in the silence.

She clapped her hands over her ears. When she pulled them away, gravel was trickling down the wall. "Did you hear someone?" Her heartbeat raced at the possibility. Would they actually have help getting out? Would she be rescued this time?

"I think so. We need to be louder. Here, take the phone and find me a spike. I'll tap it against the shovel head."

Quickly, she lit the area and scrambled down to snatch up a spike from where it leaned against the wall. When she crawled back up behind him, she patted his tight butt. "Here."

He took it from her and started banging the shovel head with it. He struck five times and stopped.

This time she definitely heard a voice, though it still sounded far away.

"Did you hear that?" He looked back at her.

"I did." Now that rescue could actually happen, she was afraid to hope. Afraid they'd move on. "Strike it again."

He did and this time they heard a distinct shout, closer now. Garrett yelled again. "In here!"

This time the voice was clearer and a low rumbling could be heard.

Garrett crawled backward out of the tunnel and the two of them moved off the pile of dirt and waited, their eyes focused on the tunnel.

"Garrett, Riley, we're coming for you. Where are you?"

That was Cole! She grabbed the spike from his hand and

banged on the shovel with all her might. "We're here!" Fear that Cole would give up collided with her excitement.

"Wait." Garrett covered her hand with his own.

The silence scared her. They were going to leave. It was too hard to find them. Her hands became clammy and she pulled hers away from Garrett's. Pressure on her left leg distracted her. Glancing down, she found Copper looking up at her, his one eyebrow higher than the other as if to say, what the hell is going on?

She scooped him up, happy to have him to hold.

"Make some noise. We need an exact location."

Before she could say anything, Garrett had grabbed the spike from her and crawled back into the tunnel. "We're here!" He banged five more times on the shovel.

"Got you. Stand back."

Once again, he shimmied out of their tunnel. He grasped her arm and pulled her back toward their camp and answered her unspoken question at his move. "They have some kind of machine."

The rumbling sounded louder the longer they waited. After a few minutes it stopped and with it her heart. They'd given up! Her eyes started to water. This couldn't be happening. Despair almost dropped her to the ground.

"Hey, what's wrong? You should be happy." He moved his hand toward her face, but Copper licked it. He chuckled.

How could he be happy? "They've given up." She tried not to break down, but the last word came out in a squeak.

He managed to get his hand past Copper and cupped her cheek. "No, they aren't giving up. They're probably talking things over based on what they've found. Just be patient a little longer. I promise, this is how it's done. Cole's a firefighter and he's going to ensure that everyone is safe."

"Cole? The forgetful, has to be his way, can't remember shit, cowboy?"

Garrett laughed loudly. "Yes. Despite all that, as a firefighter, you wouldn't want anyone else in charge."

She found it hard to believe, and it must have shown on face.

"Even if you have no faith in Cole, trust me that I know they won't give up until we're out of here. Okay?"

At his words, her breathing became easier. She did trust him. She trusted him with her life. Setting Copper down, she nodded. "Okay."

He grinned, then leaned in and kissed her. It wasn't a peck either. When he was done, she had to remind herself where she was. Shit, the man could kiss.

"We're ready." Cole's voice was clearer. "Give us more noise."

Once again, Garrett climbed up to the end of their tunnel and banged on the shovel while she held the diming light. The whole procedure happened two more times. Were they really that far in? Nervous, she turned off the light in between Garrett making noise.

Suddenly, bits of sunlight filtered in through their tunnel. They were found!

Garrett let out a real cowboy whoop before picking her up and spinning her around. When he put her down, he kissed her so tenderly she almost started to cry. He grinned. "We did it."

She wasn't sure what they'd done, but her throat was too tight to ask.

"Hey, are you there?" Cole's voice came from the other end of their tunnel.

Garrett moved to where he could be seen. "I never thought I'd be so glad to see your face, Hatcher."

Cole laughed. "Same here. Is Riley with you?"

He pulled her over and set her in front of him. "Hey, Cole."

All she could see was Cole's head. He lifted his cowboy hat and wiped his brow. "Thank God."

She couldn't say anything. Her emotions felt too close to the surface. Her last escape had been a solo endeavor that had only ended after hiking back to Chora, being careful not to be seen, discovering her unit had pulled out, and eventually being picked up by helicopter by soldiers she'd never met. Cole sounded like he seriously cared about her, a simple ranch hand.

"You think you can crawl out of there?" Cole's voice was filled with concern.

Garrett moved her to the side. "Can you dig in farther?"

"I'd rather not. It looks like there was a mudslide, but it's all dried out and weak. We had to put up three supports just to get this far. How is it on your end?"

"The same. We'll crawl out. I'm sending Riley first."

"No." She pushed in front of him. "I'm sending Copper out first. He hasn't eaten in days and has had very little to drink. He's going to need Dr. Jenna."

Cole lowered his brows. "Copper?"

She turned around and scooped up Copper. "Yes. He's my dog. Go ahead Copper. Go to Cole."

The dog didn't move a muscle except to look back at her.

"Really? I'm coming right behind you."

Garrett leaned in closer. "You need to get up there with him. He won't leave without you."

"He won't—crap." Her eyes started to water again. It must have to do with finally getting out of the godforsaken mine. Crawling up on the hill behind Copper, she nudged him. "Okay, boy. Let's go."

Just as Garrett had said, Copper walked forward checking behind him every couple steps. His loyalty to her was making it hard to keep it together. When Cole pulled Copper out, she let out a breath, not even realizing how nervous she was. The tunnel was narrow and as she brushed the side, loose dirt fell.

When she got to the opening, two men she didn't know, pulled her whole body out until she could stand. But the sunlight was so bright, she felt dizzy and covered her eyes. In the next moment she was whisked off her feet and carried to a waiting ambulance a hundred yards away. What the hell? "Put me down."

Luckily, whoever carried her, set her on the back of the ambulance. "I can walk, it's just too freaking bright."

"Get this lady some sunglasses! I need to grab Walker."

Walker? She watched the very large firefighter stride back to what looked like a mouse hole in the middle of a debris field. Someone handed her sunglasses, and she quickly put them on, even as they wrapped her in a blanket. Really? It had to be over a hundred and ten. Shrugging it off, she kept her hand over the sunglasses to watch the hole for Garrett.

Cole moved in front of the hole and spoke. She couldn't hear what he said, but he didn't move aside until the big firefighter joined him. Right. Now Garrett could come out.

"Miss, I'm Lieutenant Alvarez. Can I take a look at your arm?"

She gave the dark-haired firefighter a cursory look. "Sure." She held out her left arm and returned her gaze to the hole. *Come on Garrett. What are you waiting for?*

The man at her left arm called to someone behind her, but she didn't pay any attention. Every one of her muscles was tense with waiting. What the hell was taking so long? Did she take that long?

Suddenly, Cole and the big fire fighter jumped back and the hole disappeared.

Garrett!

Chapter Twelve

Riley jumped up and took a step forward before a hand clamped down on her. "Miss, we have to get you to the hospital. You're dehydrated and have an infected arm."

She glanced down at her arm to see the red puffiness, but quickly found the man holding her. She glared. "Take your hand off me."

"Do you understand? You need to go to the hospital." He spoke as if she was in first grade, but didn't release her.

She stepped up to him. "I'm not going anywhere until Garrett is out of that cave. Do you understand me, soldier?"

The firefighter gave her an odd look. "I do understand what you want, but we have to make sure you're treated first."

Beyond exasperated, she swore. "Get your fucking hand off me or choose which one of your balls you want to lose."

His eyes widened and his grip lessened.

She ripped her arm from him and ran back toward the hole. Before she could get close, a large meaty arm wrapped around her. "Whoa, there. Do you want to be buried too?"

At his words, her heart constricted. Buried? No, he couldn't be. Not again. She couldn't lose another person. She'd been so careful.

"Hey, don't cry. Walker's tougher than a little cave-in."

She looked up at the man that had carried her out of the hole. "Is he alive?"

He smirked. "I'd bet a million on it. He's cheated death more than once."

That was true, but what if his luck had run out?

"Want to take my bet?"

"What?" She couldn't stop staring at the wall of dirt.

"I bet he'll come out of there riding a pink unicorn, too."

Cole yelled something to the driver of the bucket loader. He wouldn't be doing that if Garrett were dead, would he?"

"Maybe even have a pair of blue bunnies on his lap."

Blue bunnies? She finally turned to look at the man who continued to keep her away. "What are you talking about?"

He blinked innocently. "About Walker getting out of that mine."

She raised her brows in doubt. "Who are you?"

"I'm Scott Mason. Best firefighter this side of the Alamo and rescuer of damsels in distress."

Seriously? Without warning, she jammed her cowboy boot onto the arch of his foot.

"Ow, now why'd you do that? Here I thought we were getting along so well."

Frustrated she hadn't done more damage to the football firefighter holding her, she yelled. "Cole!"

Cole strode to where she stood, "Mason, let her go."

"As you wish, Cap." And just like that she was released. She glared at the big man before turning on Cole. She studied him. He didn't look nervous at all. He looked like he was in his element. "Is Garrett alive?"

"Yes. He yelled from inside that he's okay. If he was hurt, he'd let us know. He knows how important it is to our operation."

Operation? For the first time she scanned the area outside

the mine. There was one fire engine, one ambulance, a front loader, and a bunch of ATVs. Her gaze moved back to the fire engine where a firefighter was giving Copper some water. Domino? She scanned what looked like a town instead of the empty desert she'd ridden to. "My horse?"

Cole shook his head. "She's the strangest horse I think we have had on Last Chance."

"But is she okay?" Why couldn't these men just answer a question?

"She's fine. From what we can tell, she used my barn for shelter and water. When I came home, she wouldn't let us near her. She kept running out into the desert, so I hopped on Samson and followed her. It wasn't until she came to this spot that she let me close. It wasn't hard to put two and two together."

The driver of the front loader yelled to Cole who held up his hand. "I need to get Garrett out now. Can I trust you to stay here and out of the way?"

She nodded. Copper and Domino were going to be fine. Now she just needed Garrett.

As Cole strode to the wall of dirt, she held her hand over the sunglasses. The light still hurt her eyes, and she wanted to see the minute Garrett was free. Only then could she relax. Only then could she leave.

It took another set of bracing before they were able to dig far enough into the mountain to expose the hole again. She held her breath as Cole approached it and yelled inside. Then he signaled Mason and the two of them stood on either side.

It took a few minutes, but finally Garrett's head could be seen. As soon as Cole and Mason pulled him out to stand, she turned and went back to the ambulance. "I'm ready to leave now."

Alvarez helped her into the back and had her lie down.

"Don't worry. Cole will make sure Garrett makes it to the hospital."

"My dog?"

"Clark will check him over, give him some electrolytes, and leave him with Cole, if that's okay?"

She nodded, too worn out to speak. It wasn't the mine or the physical hardship that had exhausted her. It was Garrett. She'd thought she'd been very careful not to make any connections with anyone, but when the hole disappeared, she knew that sickening feeling of losing someone all over again.

She'd felt it when they received word her dad had died and again when her mother passed. Though she never understood her mother, the woman was her family. She hadn't been able to help her mom or her own sister. Then it had been her unit members. She knew then it was too much. She couldn't lose anyone else. If Garrett had died after coming so close to escaping...

She closed her eyes. Never again.

Garrett pulled his truck to a stop in front of the Last Chance Ranch main house. He needed to talk to Riley. By the time he'd made it to the hospital to be checked out, she'd been released and then his family had descended upon him.

He didn't blame Cole for alerting them that he was missing, and he was happy to see them. He had hoped to see Riley for himself since Mason had told him that she had an infection in her arm. He'd been afraid of that, but it had been over twenty-four hours since they'd escaped from the mine.

Striding to the front porch and up the steps, he almost collided with the man coming outside. "Hello, Wyatt."

The black-haired, tanned cowboy halted. "Garrett. I heard about yours and Riley's rescue. You okay?"

"I'm fine. I understand we have you to thank for taking care of all the horses."

The man looked away. "There was no one else here, and to be honest, I thought this was the worst run ranch in Arizona." He finally met his gaze. "But I'm glad I was here, especially since that monsoon came through."

He clapped the man on the shoulder. "I am too. When Riley started to worry about the horses, I assured her you'd take care of them."

Wyatt rubbed the back of his neck. "I just wish I hadn't fallen asleep on the couch Friday night. I would have called Cole sooner. It wasn't until I woke up Saturday morning that I realized things were serious."

Garrett stepped back. "You didn't think something was wrong when Black Jack came back to the ranch riderless?"

"My mind was on other things and by time I got here, the horse was standing next to the lean-to by the barn, so I thought someone had saddled him and then got called away and forgot. There was nothing on him to say he'd thrown anyone or wandered off on someone. Like I said, I wasn't thinking clearly. I've been on edge ever since Gramps died. Nothing's right now. Not even me."

He studied the man. There was more to this, but he didn't have the time now to figure it out. "Well, I'm glad you did call Cole. Another day in that mine and we would have been in tough shape. So thanks. Is Riley home?"

"She is for now. I'm going to take Guinness for a ride."

Garrett nodded and moved past the man to open the screen door. He knocked.

Wyatt yelled over his shoulder. "Cole's in the kitchen. Go ahead in."

Opening the door, he strode inside and found Cole.

"I thought I heard a truck. I can't tell you how glad I am to see you." Cole's welcome seemed a bit over the top. He'd been the one to get them out of the mine after all.

"It's good to see you. Is Riley here?"

Cole moved to the fridge and pulled out a beer, silently offering him one.

He shook his head.

"She just quit on me." Cole opened the bottle and sat at the table.

"Quit? I thought she liked working here."

Cole's shoulders fell. "She wouldn't give me a reason, but I think she blames me for the mine cave-in. I should have boarded that place up years ago. I kept meaning to." He took a gulp of beer and looked at him. "Any chance you've thought about that job I offered you."

"No, I haven't." That wasn't the Riley he knew. He had to talk to her. Find out what was going on.

"Then think about it. As of today. I have no fulltime ranch hands and no ranch manager. I need both."

"Where is she?"

Cole gave him a shrewd look. "Upstairs. While you're talking, see if you can't talk her into staying."

"Believe me, I will." He spun on his heel and walked down the hall, but he took the stairs two at a time, his heart going into double time. Remembering his quick run through the house less than a week ago, he turned left at the top of the staircase.

Her door was open, and he could hear her on the phone. "I can come down on Thursday. I appreciate it."

He walked to the open door and leaned against the jamb. She sat on one of the two twin beds, her back to him and a large

Army duffle bag lay open on the floor, a few things already in it. "Going somewhere?"

She stood, spinning around to face him, her phone dropping to the bed. "Shit, Garrett. What are you doing here?"

"I came to see if you're okay. That's what teammates do after going through a tough experience. Surely you know that." He couldn't keep the sarcasm out of his voice. Everything in the room screamed she was running away, but he tried to tamp down his rising anger. There may be a logical explanation.

She looked down at her phone and picked it up, putting it in her back pocket. "Cole told me you were okay." She shrugged. "I don't know where you live, so I figured you'd be by eventually. I know you have family in town."

He strode forward, needing to be near her, but suddenly unsure of her. After the mine, he thought she had feelings for him, maybe felt as strongly as he did. "But you're packing. Cole says you quit."

"I've got a new job. This was only supposed to be temporary anyway." She flung her arm out to encompass the room, as if that explained everything.

Ire rose, but he clamped down hard. Maybe someone nearby had offered her a job. "Where?"

She picked up her utility knife and dropped it in the duffle bag. "Yuma."

"Yuma?" His mind was processing a lot faster than his heart was. "Why, Yuma?"

She shrugged. "Why not? Home is wherever I drop my bag. I told you that."

She turned back to the nightstand, but he grabbed her by the shoulders and made her face him. "So why not Wickenburg?"

She frowned. "Wickenburg? There's a job available there?"

"No, but it's where I live. If you have to leave here then

come live with me. It's a big house. I could give you your own space."

Her gaze left his. "I can't."

"Why not? I thought we got along pretty well in the mine."

She shrugged off his hands. "That was different. Luckily, life isn't like being buried alive."

He fisted his hands at his side. "It's also not meant to run away from. I know you felt something." He held up his hand as she opened her mouth, "and don't try to tell me it was just the situation that made us seem close."

She looked down. "No. It wasn't."

"Then why are you intent on leaving here? Leaving me?"

She walked around the second bed, obviously wanting space between them. The action cutting into him more than she knew. "You wouldn't understand."

"Try me." He folded his arms across his chest. There was nothing she could say that would convince him this was right. Not when he knew she was right for him.

She waved her hand between them. "I don't do this. I don't connect with people. It doesn't work for me."

Baffled, he shook his head. "What do you mean?"

"I mean the whole rescue, people looking for me, the dog, you. I don't want people caring about me. I don't want to care about people. It only leads to pain. I've had enough pain. I can't do it again. It will kill me."

Now this was the woman he'd been trapped with. "It doesn't have to lead to pain. It can lead to joy and happiness."

She shook her head. "Not for me. It always leads to pain. Everyone dies on me. It's better not to connect. Then it doesn't matter. No one matters. I don't matter."

He strode around the bed and cupped her face. "But you do matter. You matter to me."

For a moment, a second, he saw it in her dark eyes. She did feel for him. It was there. Just as his heart jumped at the knowledge, she pulled away. "No, I don't. You will have a better life without me in it. You know, better than anyone, I'm a mess. You don't need that. You deserve a hero's wife. Not a screwed-up vet who can't even keep a gold fish alive."

Her rejection hurt, but still he tried. "You have it backwards. I'm the one that's scarred and you're the hero. You're the soldier who defended our country. What have I done? I defended houses and screwed up. I don't deserve you, but I want you anyway."

She shook her head. "Don't you see? I can't care. I suck at it. I've tried. I failed my mother. I couldn't save my sister. I led my men into an ambush. Everyone is better without me. I have to go. You'll find someone better than me."

"There is no one better *for* me." He stared at her, the pain in his chest growing even as he tried to deny what was happening.

"Yes, you will. You belong here. With friends and family. I don't. I don't do friends and family." She brushed by him and moved to the dresser and opened a drawer. Pulling out three pair of jeans, she threw them in the duffle bag and pointed. "This is my life. This is what I choose. I can't lose another or I'll lose what sanity I have left."

Nausea started in the pit of his stomach as hurt and anger churned inside him. His voice rose of its own accord and he didn't care. "You can't live your life avoiding loss, it's impossible."

She rounded on him. "Really? Then why haven't you found another dog? I'll tell you why. Because you can't handle loving something and losing it. Try that seven times over only with people. Then you can tell me what I can avoid and what I can't!"

"You think I haven't lost people? I've lost comrades to

alcohol, fire, and cancer. I gave my heart to two women only to have them walk away because of my body, yet still I opened my heart again. This time to you."

She backed up a step, shaking her head. "Why? Why would you do that?"

He advanced on her. "Because the reward is worth all the heartache that came before. The culmination makes everything else worth it. Human connection is the reason for living and loving others is being alive."

She stared at him, her mouth slightly parted, her brown eyes round with denial and confusion.

"I'll ask you one more time. Will you stay? Will you give us a chance?"

He held his breath, the small flame of hope refusing to go out.

Riley's gaze moved from one of his eyes to the other, and the flame grew, but when she looked away, the punch to his gut almost doubled him over. "I can't."

He fisted his hands to keep from lashing out, the pain in his chest far worse than any he'd experienced with anyone else. Turning on his heel, he strode out, down the stairs and outside, letting the screen door slam behind him.

She'd been right about one thing, when it came to the scarred mess his body was, he hadn't found the right woman. But he'd been dumb enough to think if he found a woman to accept his body, she'd also love him.

How wrong he was.

~~*~~

Riley checked the room she'd lived in for well over a year and a half. In a way, she was glad that Annette and Ed were still on their cruise. She didn't like goodbyes. Besides, she looked like shit after crying herself to sleep the last two nights.

Cole had enlisted Wyatt's help temporarily. Apparently, the morose, by-the-book cowboy had given his stamp of approval to the ranch. The man confirmed what she'd always thought, one had to be drop-dead handsome to be allowed to work at Last Chance. It was too bad the sorrow in his pale green eyes made it hard to look at him. Maybe the ranch could rescue him like it rescued horses. She wished him luck, especially working for Cole.

However, her boss *had* offered to keep Domino until she could get settled. For some reason, he seemed to feel guilty about the mine cave-in, though why she had no idea. She could leave the paint at Last Chance forever, but she'd grown too attached to the horse and now that Domino had saved her life, she couldn't let her go.

Now all she had to do is say goodbye to Copper and she could move on. She didn't want to, but he belonged to Whisper. Besides, he reminded her of Garrett and whether she'd wanted to or not, she'd fallen for the man. As usual, she'd ruined it. She was seriously messed up. It was better not to mess other people's lives up. It was the least she could do for him and Copper.

Zipping up her duffle, she hoisted it over her shoulder and headed out. At the doorway she looked back. "You coming? Whisper will be here soon."

Copper jumped off the made bed and trotted over to her.

"You'll be very happy with Whisper and Trace. She'll take much better care of you than I can." She snorted. "Can't even take care of myself."

Striding down the stairs and outside, she dumped her duffle in the backseat.

Copper hopped in before she could close the door.

"I don't think so, buddy." She lifted him out and slammed the door shut before he could jump back in.

He was looking no worse for wear. At least he'd had a few days to recover before Whisper came to pick him up. Whisper would have her head if he looked malnourished. Dr. Jenna had made a special trip out when she heard about the cave-in and gave Copper a thorough examination. He was pronounced in good health.

Now she could hand him over to Whisper with a clear conscience.

Though it was morning, it was already hot, so she walked over to the shade of the mesquite tree and sat on the ground to wait for Whisper. Copper followed her and immediately tried to lick her face. "Really. Can't you just sit?"

Copper instantly dropped his butt to the ground and looked at her expectantly.

"You've got to be shitting me. All this time and all I had to do is tell you to sit?"

The dog's tail wagged even as he lifted his one eyebrow.

"Hell, I'm going to miss you. Come here."

He jumped in her lap and attempted to lick her again. She laughed, rolling back and protecting her face with her hands. Silly dog.

The sound of a truck approaching had her sitting up. From her vantage point, all she could see was dust. Rising to her feet, she shaded her eyes then looked down at Copper who stood next to her waiting. "She's here."

The words barely made it out of her tightening throat. Since when had leaving a place become so hard? First, it was Garrett, then the going away party they threw her last night, now Copper. It just proved she'd put off leaving for too long. She'd remember that next time. Never stay longer than a year.

Whisper's truck pulled to a stop, and she jumped out before the dust had settled. She strode over to where they stood waiting for her. "I don't understand why you want to give me Copper."

That was Whisper. Right to the point. "Because he's yours."

"We don't own animals. They choose us."

She very much doubted that the gerbils she had when she was little had chosen her since they'd escaped into the walls of the house, but she wasn't about to argue with the woman. "Then I guess he chose you when you spotted him on the side of the road."

Whisper shook her head. "I don't think so. Come here, Copper."

The dog looked at Whisper and then up at her. "Go ahead. You remember her, right?"

Copper looked back at Whisper and walked over. Whisper sat on the ground getting eye to eye with the dog. "Good dog." She rubbed him behind the ear, and he sat.

Now why didn't he lick Whisper's face? Whisper was gorgeous. Her skin was always tan and she had straight, thick black hair that Riley envied. What did her mom say? We always want what we don't have? Wow, she hadn't thought of something her mom taught her in years.

She waited patiently for Whisper to finish with Copper. She had no idea what the two were doing, but she knew better than to disturb whatever was going on.

Whisper spoke to Copper. "I understand." Slowly, she rose. "I can't take him."

"What?" Her heart started jumping up and down, but she kept her brain functioning. "What do you mean you can't take him? You found him."

Whisper shook her head. "No. He needs you. I can't take him away from you. There was a bond developed during your trauma. It's not something that can ever be broken."

"But I don't know anything about dogs except they don't like mints."

"You'll learn. Garrett will help you."

Okay, Whisper understanding animals was crazy enough, but she had no idea what she was talking about when it came to people. "Garrett can't help. I'm leaving for Yuma, right now."

"You can't go."

Oh, for shit's sake. "Why?"

"Copper needs Garrett, too. So do you. And Garrett needs you and Copper. This bond that was forged in the mine will never break no matter where you go."

"You've got to be kidding. Are you trying to tell me that if Copper and I go to Yuma, we'll be miserable for the rest of our lives and Garrett will be miserable for the rest of his life?"

"Yes." Whisper didn't even blink as she made that pronouncement, and it scared the shit out of Riley.

Still, she shook her head. "I can't stay. I have a job in Yuma."

Whisper grinned. "But you have a life here. Don't be an ass. What happened in that mine is a part of you all now."

Great, after three days of avoiding thinking about her time in the mine, Whisper had to bring it up twice. She scowled.

Whisper jerked her head in the direction of the road leading away from Last Chance. "Take Copper and go to Garrett. He needs you both and you both need him."

Again, her heart wanted to listen to Whisper. Fuck, did the woman have some kind of magic? "I already closed that door."

"Then open it."

"And if he slams it in my face? Then what?"

Whisper shrugged. "Then you go to Yuma. Now I have to get back to my husband. We're supposed to pick up a birthday cake for Old Billie."

"Wait, what? Your husband?"

Whisper opened the door of her truck. "Yes, Trace and I married in Las Vegas." Her face softened. "Uncle Joey was his best man. We're all legal now."

Riley strode up to the truck. "But you didn't say anything last night."

"It doesn't change anything except now I get to call him husband." Whisper closed her door and started the engine. Then the window came down. "Take Copper to Garrett. Don't break the bond." With those final words, she drove out of the yard.

Riley watched the truck until it disappeared. Whisper was crazy. She knew animals but not people.

Besides, Riley didn't even know where Garrett lived, though a stop at the fire station to see Cole would take care of that.

No, she was going to Yuma.

She looked down at Copper. He met her gaze, one eyebrow higher than the other and cocked his head. "The shit you get me into."

Garrett swore as the drill bit snapped. He was an idiot for trying to build a porch in the middle of the summer heat by himself, but the promise of shade sooner rather than later was too hard to ignore.

Wiping the sweat from his eyes with his discarded t-shirt, he dropped it on the sawhorse and went into the shed for another drill bit. He might have to take Mason up on his offer to bring over some of the firehouse guys to help. His dad had offered to stay and work with him, but he didn't want him working in the heat. It was already close to ninety and climbing.

Opening his drill bit case, he paused at the sound of a truck pulling into his dirt driveway. Damn, his shirt was in front of the house. He'd bought the home as much for its potential as for acres of land that kept him from the eyes of prying neighbors. So, who the hell was here?

Standing in the dark shed, he peered out to see who had arrived. When Riley stepped out of her truck, he sucked in his breath. The sun glinted off her fiery red hair, beneath what looked like a new white cowboy hat. She wore a simple white t-shirt and her usual blue jeans. All dressed and ready for her new job.

The thought brought back his anger. What the hell was she doing here? Had she decided to say goodbye and rub in the fact she was leaving? If so, he could make this pretty quick.

He ignored the fact he had no shirt on and strode out to see what she wanted. "What are you doing here?"

"Hello to you too."

He moved to where his tape measure sat next to his t-shirt. "If you've come to say goodbye, well goodbye."

Using the tape measure, he ran it from one post to the other, then went back to a two by four and wrote the measurement down.

"No, I came because of Copper."

Copper? He looked up to see her open the passenger door of the truck and Copper hopped down. Damn, if he didn't miss the little guy. "What about Copper?"

"Whisper said he needs you."

As if to prove the point, Copper ran to him and pawed at his leg. Shit, he couldn't ignore him and not pet him. "Are you trying to tell me your abandoning your dog like you are me?"

She grimaced. "Shit, I deserve that, but no, I'm not abandoning him. I'm not abandoning anyone. Whisper said there was an unbreakable bond between you and Copper."

He'd never met this Whisper, and now he wasn't sure he

wanted to. She sounded like one of those people who believed in crystals. Not that he had a problem with that, it just wasn't his thing.

He crouched down and gave Copper most of his attention. At least the dog was straight forward with his affection. "What are you talking about, Riley? If you didn't come to say goodbye and you didn't come to drop your dog off with me before you left then why are you here?"

When she didn't answer, he finally looked at her. "Well."

"I…I…"

Did the woman not realize that just standing in front of him made the pain of losing her worse? "Damn it, spit it out."

"I love you. Okay?"

He froze, his whole body stuck in time.

"I can't help it. I didn't want it to happen, but Whisper says we formed a bond and it can't be broken. She said we would all be miserable if I tried to break it. Fuck, I'm so tired of being miserable. I don't want to avoid life anymore. What the hell have I been surviving for if it wasn't to live? I'm a complete basket case and a total mess, but for some reason I still want to be happy. That didn't happen until you."

His lungs finally sucked air in, and he took a moment to digest what she said. She loved him and didn't want to throw that away? But could he trust her with his heart?

"So, you'll be staying at Last Chance?"

She shook her head and his anger returned. "So, you're still going to Yuma."

She shook her head again.

"Well, which is it?"

She walked to her truck and opened the back door. Pulling her duffle bag out, she hoisted it over her shoulder. "Copper and I would like to stay here. If you'll have us."

His heart skipped a beat. He put the tape measure down and walked to her. "Let me get this straight. You're saying that you love me and want to move in with me?"

"Copper, too." She looked around the property. "I can keep Domino at Last Chance until I can build her a place here."

His hope burst into flame in his chest, but still he hesitated. "What changed? I can't believe it was Whisper and this bonding in the mine thing."

She gave him a small smile. "It wasn't. In fact, I'd avoided thinking of the mine. No nightmares either, and then she had to go and bring it up, making it sound like it was fate or voodoo or some vortex magic."

She paused, as if looking for the words to explain. "I really thought I'd figured out how to survive, but I was just existing, avoiding any strong feelings. I was afraid. But as I drove away from Last Chance, I remembered how I felt in the mine when it first caved in. My worst fear had been realized, being buried alive again. But you being there gave me strength, calmed me, and supported my hope. You rescued me long before the cavalry arrived."

He couldn't hold onto his anger at her words. "You gave me all that as well."

She placed her hand over his heart, her touch cool against his warm skin. "I know I'm messed up and not much of a prize, but I think I can get better with you. If you'll have me."

He grasped her hand in his and held it to his scarred chest. "I'd be honored." Gazing into her deep brown eyes, he saw her truth. She'd laid bare all that she was for him. "I love you, Riley." Pulling her to him, he gave her his love in a kiss.

Suddenly, she pulled back. "Oh." She looked down and laughed. "I think someone is jealous."

He smiled, letting her go and scooped up Copper. "Welcome to the family, boy."

The dog licked his face. "Ugh."

Snatching up his t-shirt he wiped his face to the sultry sound of Riley's laughter. It filled his heart to hear it. Keeping the dog under one arm, he held out his other to his woman. "Let me show you around our place."

She took his arm and gave Copper a pet. "We'd like that. We'd like that a lot."

Epilogue

Riley softly smiled as the car meandered through the back roads northwest of Prescott, towering pines giving the roads a magical forest quality. In less than a month, her whole world had changed for the better. More like it got flipped upside down!

Instead of rambling about alone in the world avoiding relationships of any kind, she had a man who loved her, a dog who couldn't be more than twenty-feet away from her, a horse that was loyal to her, and friends at Last Chance. Though she technically still worked there, even that relationship had changed.

And now she had a family.

"Does that smile mean that meeting my family wasn't the ordeal you'd expected it to be?"

She looked over at Garrett as he drove. "I know you told me they'd be happy to meet me, but they weren't anything like I expected. Your dad, is well, I'm surprised he ever retired from the fire department. He has so much energy. He reminded me of that firefighter, Mason, who pulled me from the mine."

"I never thought about it, but there is a bit of resemblance in personality. Might be why, in my time at the station, we always got along. Though you must admit, my dad has more hair."

She laughed. "Yes, he does, and he's very handsome with that white at his temples."

201

He glanced at her. "I guess handsome runs in the family."

She squeezed his thigh. "Don't be getting a big ego on me now. Besides, I haven't met your brother yet, so I'm not sure." She smirked. "Actually, I was just thinking that you take after your mom. Now I understand why you can be a cowboy and yet still respect my abilities despite being a woman."

"Despite?" He lowered his brows.

"Yes." She waved her hand. "I know you told me your mom was the rancher, but I didn't really believe it until now. What a kick to see her running the whole show, and your sister makes a great manager."

"They have that place running like a well-oiled machine, but I still don't understand why you say I respect your abilities *despite* being a woman." He slowed the truck and turned onto a smaller road, the pavement barely hanging on.

He wouldn't understand. Her military experience had made her expect certain attitudes from men, resentment, indifference, distrust. Though there had been those who respected her, they were few in numbers.

"What are you thinking?"

Somehow, he always knew when to interrupt her thoughts. "I'm thinking that your upbringing may make it hard for you to understand what it's like to be a woman in a male-dominated career."

"How can you—"

"Wait, I wasn't finished. I think this because you grew-up respecting your mom and her leadership. Many men don't have that at such a young age, so even if they want to, even if they have to, taking direction from a woman is hard."

He grinned. "So you're saying I'm unique."

She snorted. "In more ways than one. Your most unique quality is that you can put up with me."

He chuckled. "There is that." His smile suddenly left and the truck rolled to a stop in the middle of the road.

"What is it?"

He pointed to the left. "That's where we were staging for the fire. It was right here where I saw the little girl in her family's car."

She looked around. They were in the middle of nowhere, the closest town miles away. They hadn't seen another car since two roads back. She hoped that didn't mean what it seemed to mean. "Are you sure this is the spot? I know it's been five years, but this doesn't appear to have been burned."

He put his window down letting the fresh air in, which was much cooler than the Sonoran Desert. They could hear birds, but little else. It was peaceful.

"The fire didn't reach here while I was working it. From what my team told me, it continued north."

Copper stuck his nose between Garrett's seat and the window.

For some reason the dog loved it when the truck windows were down. Supposedly that was normal. "And you never asked them about the community of shacks?"

He shook his head. "You're the only one who knows what motivated me to risk my life that day. If the fire had jumped the break, which it could if the winds picked up in the right direction, then there's another road about seven miles east as the crow flies that would have been the fallback position. After that was a full town."

"Did the town burn?"

"No."

If she had been seriously wounded trying to save another soldier, she would have to know if it had been worth it. Hell, even when she wasn't injured and helped a soldier, she damn well made sure she found out if the man made it. "Okay, I had to face my fears in that shitty old mine. It's time to face yours."

His hands gripped the steering wheel like a man holds a grenade when the pin has been pulled, but he didn't say a word.

"You said you never checked because you feared your sacrifice was in vain. What if it was? What if all those shacks are gone when we get there?"

"Eight."

"Eight what?

Shacks." He swallowed hard, his Adam's Apple giving away his tension.

She wanted to help him like he'd helped her. She wasn't as good at it, but she was learning. He had been both calm and at times commanding. "Okay, say all eight shacks are gone, burnt to cinders. What then? Will you give up on life? Will you stop working on your home? Will you kick me out?"

He snapped his head around to look at her. "No."

She'd hoped she knew the answer, but it was reassuring to hear. "We would have never met if you didn't try to save those buildings. You would have still been up here or out of state fighting wildfires, while I worked at Last Chance." She felt the blood drain from her face. "I would have been alone in that mine."

He let go of the steering wheel and pulled her to him. "Don't even think about that."

She took a deep breath, his comforting embrace always a balm to her ruptured psyche, but she could handle the "what if," since it hadn't actually happened. She pulled away. "I'm okay. It was just a thought. But it didn't happen that way. Why? Because you needed to get away from up here, to start a new life. So whether those shacks are still there or not, has your life been a nightmare?"

"At first, yes, but I understand what you're saying." He hesitated, then he gave her a lopsided grin. "In other words, it doesn't matter if they still stand or not." He stepped on the brake and put the truck into reverse.

Oh, no. He wasn't getting out of it that easy. She grabbed his arm. "Whoa there, cowboy. I need you to step back and bring out that brave firefighter I know is hiding somewhere in there."

"Hiding? I'm not hiding. You just explained why this is a wasted trip."

She pointed up the road and took command of the situation. "Garrett, you put this truck back into drive and get your tail up there or you're cleaning out the head for the rest of the year. I'm not having any soldier going AWOL on my watch."

He let out a deep breath. "Yes, ma'am. You're right." Slowly, as if against his will, he changed gears and started the truck forward at less than 20mph.

It was on the tip of her tongue to give him a hard time about driving like an old man, but she reconsidered. He was doing what he promised. If he could have patience with her, she could have patience with him.

They continued for almost half a mile before he spoke. "Here's the beginning of the firebreak."

She looked out the front windshield to his side of the road which had brightened considerably. There was nothing but weeds and grasses and a few short shrubs from the road to about four hundred feet into the forest and then it looked like an abandoned nightmare.

Once towering ponderosa pines were skinny black sentinels ready to fall, some already leaning on each other. At their base were green shrubs, bushes, and tiny trees, seemingly oblivious to the threat of the delicate monsters above them.

They continued slowly up the road, the bird song having stopped. The burned landscape seemed to go on forever, but that may have been because he drove so slow. As far as she could see, the black burnt wood covered the landscape, most standing straight like soldiers at attention but many others littering the forest floor. The heat of the fire had to have been intense.

"If they are still here, they should be around the next bend on your side of the road." Garrett's voice was low, his dread clear.

She held her breath as she strained to peek between the trees on the right side of the crumbling pavement of the road. Halfway through the curve, she saw a wood wall. *Please, let it be part of a building and not the remnants of a fire.*

The truck rolled ahead revealing a full structure and then another. There were even cars parked outside them and children were climbing a tree in one of the yards. She let out a breath and gazed at Garrett.

His face remained serious as he took in every detail.

The years since the fire had added three more homes from what she could see, though calling them "homes" was being generous. It looked like a refugee camp in the middle of the towering evergreens. She understood now, why this had been so important to him that he'd risk his life.

A ball rolled into the street in front of them and Garrett stopped the truck. The young man chasing it also stopped at the side of the road. Copper barked.

"That's not for you." Garrett waved the boy across. "Go ahead."

The young man gave him a wave and grabbed up what looked like a dodge ball. He returned to a common area, if pine needles could be called that, and what appeared to be a game of soccer with two carboard boxes set up as their goals.

She put her hand on his thigh again and smiled. "They're all here."

He nodded. "They are. And then some."

A knock on her window startled both her and Copper, who ran across the backseat to her side of the truck and barked again. Turning, she found a middle-aged man in a Phoenix Suns t-shirt standing there. She put her window down, and he set his hand on the door. "You folks lost?"

She smiled at him. "No, sir. We just wanted to see how the forest looked after that fire five years ago."

The man shook his head. "I was here for that one. They had us all evacuate. Never thought I'd see this place again." He jerked his head toward the small community. "Some of them don't know how lucky we were. Those Hot Shots came in and kept that fire back there." He pointed to the other side of the street, looking at it as if he still couldn't believe it had stayed away.

She smirked. "So they're responsible for saving your homes?"

The man returned his attention to her. "Damn straight they did. Not just our homes but our lives. These are all we have. When they made us evacuate, we went to a shelter. My wife, Elli, spent the whole day and night praying for us and the firefighters. I was more worried about what happened when they closed the shelter, and we had to find somewhere else to live. I can't thank those Hot Shots enough."

Pride filled her for what Garrett had done. "As a matter of fact, you—"

"You can be assured they know." Garrett interrupted. "That's their job to protect people and save property if they can. I know they are happy to do that. So you were able to move back. Did everyone?"

The man nodded. "We had nowhere else to go. You could have blown me over with a dust devil when we found this place still standing." He shook his head again as if he still had a hard time believing it. "Me and my wife, we're on social security now and we could move into town, but this is home. Where are you folks from?"

Garrett replied. "I'm living in the north valley in Wickenburg."

"And I'm an Army brat, so I guess you could say I'm from everywhere."

The man looked back at his home. "You need to put down roots. It's a good feeling." He turned back to her. "You two figuring on driving the whole road? If you are, I hope you got a full tank of gas. That fire went on forever. Hopped this road where they hadn't cleared further up. Not a pretty sight."

Shit, Garrett's team had seriously saved the little community. She looked at Garrett who had an odd look on his face, but he didn't say anything. She faced the man again. "No, I think we'll drive a little farther then turn back."

The man patted the truck windowsill. "Good idea. Much prettier sights to see closer to Prescott. You have yourselves a nice day."

"You too. I'm so glad your homes were spared all that." She pointed to the other side of the road.

The man nodded then strolled back to where his wife had come out, obviously curious about who he was talking to.

Riley looked at Garrett. "Are you okay?"

"I'm very okay. Thank you for making me come here."

She grinned at him as the truck started forward, a little faster than before. "You didn't want him to know you were one of the Hot Shots that saved his home. Why?"

"I'm glad I was able to complete the firebreak, but it was a team effort. Twenty of us made that successful, not just me. It's better that he be thankful to all Hot Shots. They put their lives on the line every time they go out. I don't want anyone thinking of just me when they think about Hot Shots. Besides, I'm not a firefighter anymore."

Her heart filled with warmth for the man she'd fallen in love with in the dark. "Maybe, but you're still a Hot Shot in my book."

He placed his hand on hers. "My sacrifice led me in a different direction than I expected, and I'm glad it did. I found you. I'm content that I —Holy shit." His final word came out in a breath.

She'd been looking at him, but at his sudden swear, she turned forward. Her heart sank at the sight. They had come to the top of a ridge where the firebreak had stopped and as far as the eye could see it was a mix of burn and new growth.

It was a metaphor for both of them, only she had a good feeling that their growth would be a lot faster than the land before them. "I think we've seen all we need to see here. Let's go back."

He nodded and turned the truck around.

"Wait." Unbelting her seatbelt as he stopped, she got out and closed the door behind her to keep Copper inside. She stepped to the side of the road.

"What is it?"

She smiled and called over her shoulder. "It's life."

The other truck door closed and Garrett joined her.

"Where?" His gaze was on the horizon.

She pointed to the hundreds of wildflowers dotting the ground at their feet. The unusually wet summer had been kind. "There. See him. It's a bee. Oh, and there's another one." As she scanned the pretty yellow blooms, she found more bees. "My mom used to say that where there are bees there is life because they pollinate the plants."

Garrett put his arms around her from behind and rested his head on her shoulder. "If they are up here, I'm sure they are all over this terrain. It's taking time, but years from now, you won't even know there was a fire here."

She leaned back against him. "And maybe in those years, our pasts will be the same, still there, but from which our life can bloom."

He turned her in his arms. "Is my soldier waxing poetic?"

She grinned. "Oh, for shit's sake, don't count on it."

He laughed. "Good, because I'm terrible at poetry."

"I don't need someone who understands poetry. I just want a handsome, hot, firefighting cowboy who promises to always come to my rescue."

His grey-blue eyes softened as he gazed at her. "I promise. And will you always come to my rescue?"

At his words, her love for him seemed to fill her whole body. "I promise."

A bark from inside the truck had them both turning. She chuckled. "I think that means that Copper promises, too."

He looked back at her. "Then I guess that makes us a unit."

A new unit. A new family. A new life. "Absolutely." Wrapping her arms around his neck, she sealed their promises with a kiss.

The End

To see where it all began, read on for an excerpt of Cowboy's Match (Poker Flat #2) Cole and Lacey's story.

Chapter One

Cole Hatcher ignored the yellow and orange streaks of the Arizona sunset and focused on the same colors rising from the burning building as flames moved with the breeze. He spoke into the radio. "Move the two and a half inch to the northwest corner."

Two firefighters lugged the hose toward the base of the fire at the edge of the partially constructed building. Not more than fifteen feet away was a pile of old barn wood just waiting to ignite.

Stepping back toward the engine, Cole received a nod from Mason, the fire engine monitor, before speaking into the radio again. "Tanker, is the dry hydrant hooked yet?"

"Almost." The reply was not the answer Cole wanted. They would need more water than an engine and tanker could provide, and the chance of the winds picking up once the sun disappeared were better than a horse getting loose through an open gate.

As if on cue, the whinny of several frightened horses in the nearby barn caused him to tense. There was no way he would let the fire spread that way.

The radio clicked before a firefighter's voice came through. "We're hooked."

Cole breathed easier. As long as he had water, he could put this baby out. "Good. Stay with the tanker. I'll need someone to come over here and grab the one and a half inch with Clark." He watched as Clark unwound the hose, already heading toward the construction site that hid behind the smoke and flames of the fire's onslaught.

Glancing back to where the tanker was parked thirty yards away, Cole swore. "What the hell?" Coming up the hill along the dirt road his trucks had just rolled in on, were at least a half dozen golf carts filled with naked people.

He stifled a laugh. What'd they think this was? A campfire? A Wild West show? Did they plan to make s'mores? This would be a story to tell at the firehouse for sure. Still, as with all spectators to a disaster, it wasn't safe for them to be there. He silently wished he had a radio to communicate with the owner, who had enough sense to keep the resort guests from getting any closer.

For over a year, he'd been curious about the Poker Flat Nudist Resort, but Clark had been chosen to give the fire extinguisher class to all the employees before the resort opened three months ago, and Cole had no official reason to come check it out. Fighting a fire wasn't a good way to learn about a place. Whatever this new construction was, it was toast. His concern was with the barn and the horses and which way the wind would blow next.

An explosion from the fire shook the ground as flames shot into the air. "Shit." What the hell did they have in that unfinished building? The two men with the smaller hose lost their footing and fell, but since they hadn't made it to the fire yet, they were unharmed.

He'd be damned if he'd put his men in harm's way when no lives were at stake.

He turned toward the owner and motioned her closer, then faced the burning construction site. As the sky behind the fire turned a dull pink, the breeze picked up, changing the direction of the flames toward the open desert. Good for the horses, but not for wildfire potential. It'd been the driest summer on record. October temperature highs had finally dropped below triple digits and the nights were already getting cold, but there had been no rain during monsoon season.

Cole spoke into the radio again. "I need the two and half inch to lay down a curtain between the building and the open desert on your side."

"Got it." The two firefighters adjusted their hose and started a continual spray, wetting and cooling the area toward the open desert even as the men with the one-and-a-half-inch hose moved in to cover the fire base.

"Lieutenant, you wanted us?" The female voice had him turning around.

He'd forgotten he'd called over the owner. At least she and the cowboy with her were dressed. "You need to get those people out of here. I can't control the fire's embers and right now the wind is picking up."

The tall man nodded. "I'll take care of that." He immediately strode toward the golf cart brigade.

Cole turned his attention to the woman. "I've got my men focused on keeping the fire from spreading to your barn or out into the desert. A wildfire would be catastrophic, but we won't be able to save the building."

She waved her hand as if it meant little to her. "I'm not worried about the building as long as everyone is safe."

"Have you accounted for all your employees and guests?"

"Yes."

Another explosion had Cole turning away to check on his men. A voice came across his radio. "What the fuck is in here? A chemical lab?"

Cole frowned. He'd never thought of how convenient it would be to have a meth lab out at a nudist resort. He'd make sure the police investigated the place in case there had been illegal activity.

He looked at the owner. "How many more explosions should we expect?"

She frowned. "We had one before you arrived, that's what alerted me to the fire, but there shouldn't be anything that would explode over there. The plywood for the roof was completed, but they hadn't even set the windows in yet. All that was there was whatever the construction crew left."

"Do you have electricity out there yet?"

She shook her head.

Shit. "Gasoline for their generator." He spoke into his radio again. "Possible gas containers."

A gust of wind compounded his problems and he quickly repositioned his men. A siren could barely be heard in the distance, but the red and blue lights of a sheriff department car reflected far into the desert. About time they got here.

Cole spared a glance to where the golf carts had been parked and was relieved to see only a few left, but he scowled as a young woman with golden hair moved toward him and the owner, a tray of food and drinks in her hands. Shit, didn't these people realize this was a working fire? This was dangerous!

A third explosion rocked the ground and he spun in time to see a gust of wind pick up the roiling flames and throw them toward his men. He pressed the button on his radio. "Fall back!"

One man stumbled backward, catching his foot on the old barn wood and lost his grip on the hose. The other firefighter struggled with it before he went down too.

"Fuck." Cole sprinted to his men, pulling them back by their coats as the flames licked at their boots. The barn wood caught, feeding the fire.

Once his men were out of harm's way, he tackled the flailing line. A loose hose was a danger in its own right.

"Lieutenant, do you want us on the wood pile?" The question came through his radio.

Cole slammed his body onto the hose before replying, "Negative. Keep that curtain up."

The two firefighters that had been blown down regained their feet and grabbed the hose. "Thanks, Lieutenant."

He released his hold. "Pull back and soak that pile. If the wind shifts again, I don't want the barn catching."

The men nodded.

Cole turned around and strode back to the engine. The two women were still there. This wasn't a movie. Didn't they have any common sense?

After checking with Mason to be sure the water pressure was steady, he approached his audience, irritation growing at the petite stature of the blonde. Someone so delicate didn't belong at a working fire, but like the owner, at least she had clothes on. "Ladies, you need to get back." He pointed to the rise the golf carts had congregated on earlier.

The blonde smiled. "Selma sent over churros and iced tea for your men in case they need something."

Cole's blood froze. *That voice.* He studied the woman and his heart stumbled inside his chest. Her shapely figure proved she'd grown into a delectably curvy woman as he'd always expected she would, but her face was almost the same, just more refined. "Lacey Winters?"

Her brows furrowed and her button nose wrinkled as she peered back at him. Had he really changed so much in eight years? Yeah, probably. He'd been a bean pole the last he'd seen her...the night he broke it off with her.

She gave up trying to figure out who he was. "I'm sorry. Do I know you?"

He should let it go. No need to dredge up the past. He had a fire to control.

His pulse went into overdrive. Another fire. It couldn't be coincidence. He scowled at her. "You should. I'm Cole, Cole Hatcher."

Even in the reflection of the flames, her face turned pasty white and he kicked himself for revealing his identity. All he needed now was a fainting woman to contend with.

"You two know each other?" The other woman leaned on one hip, her concern for Lacey evident in the look she gave him.

At the owner's voice, Lacey recovered her color. Actually, her face changed from white to an angry flush in a matter of seconds. It reminded him of a flashover.

"Not that I want to know him." Lacey handed the tray over to the owner and stepped up to him. She poked her index finger into his chest. Hard. "So, Cole Hatcher. Are you going to accuse me of setting this fire? After all, I'm here, on the same property. It's not like you need evidence or anything. Feel free to assume the worst. I'm sure it helps to justify the way you treated me." She pulled back as if touching him made her feel sick. "Good luck with that." Turning on her heel, she stalked off, her hips swaying enticingly until he remembered where he was and who he was looking at.

"So *you're* the one who broke her heart." The owner studied him briefly then set the tray on the ground and followed after Lacey.

Shit.

Lacey didn't have a destination in mind. She didn't even see the dirt road she walked on. All she could see was Cole Hatcher, or rather the new and improved Cole Hatcher. He'd grown even taller and had filled out like a pro football player. What right did he have to look that good?

"Lacey, wait." Kendra's voice stopped her.

She didn't want to wait. She wanted to get as far from Cole as she could. That was why she'd applied for the job at Poker Flat in the first place. But Kendra was her boss.

"Lacey." Kendra grabbed her arm. "Were you planning to walk into the ravine?"

She looked at her boss blankly before refocusing on her surroundings in the growing darkness. Shoot. She'd almost walked right off the road.

She returned her gaze to Kendra and shook her head, her eyes watering at her near miss. She shouldn't let Cole affect her so much. She was supposed to be over him by now.

Kendra looped her arm in hers. "Come on. Let's let the firefighters do their job and you can tell me all about it."

Lacey swallowed the lump in her throat. "I'd rather not."

"That wasn't a request." Kendra tugged on her arm and she gave in. Her boss was twice her size and tough. Besides, Lacey owed her an explanation. Her broken heart and arson charge had been the two deciding factors for getting hired. Kendra only hired misfits and at first Lacey had appeared too perfect.

She sniffed. Heck, she was anything but perfect.

"So he's the one who broke your heart, isn't he?" Kendra didn't waste time getting to the point.

"Yes."

"I thought you said he was a cowboy and lived in Orson, Arizona."

Lacey pulled up her memory of the young man she'd fallen head over heels for. He'd been six feet tall as a high school senior and as thin as any wrangler, but even then his hard chin had given him a more mature look. Her weakness, though, had been his eyes. Cole Hatcher had always had the kindest green eyes she'd ever gazed into.

"Lacey?"

"Yes, he is, he was, I don't know. I have no idea what he's doing here or why he's a firefighter." Her stomach tensed. The last time they were at a fire together, he held her close as her parents' carriage house went up in smoke.

Kendra steered her toward her own casita. "I think we'd better have this conversation at your place."

Lacey stopped, forcing Kendra to halt. "We can't do that. We have guests and they will all be in the main building asking questions, needing food and attention."

"Of course they will, and Wade and Selma can take care of them. You and I are going to your casita." Kendra tugged her into walking again.

She sighed. She'd finally forgotten about Cole, except for the dull ache of her bruised heart. She'd moved on, gone to college, done what was right, as she always had...except he'd ignored that fact when he decided to agree with the rest of the town.

Kendra stepped back when they reached the door to her casita.

Pulling her resort keyring from the pocket in her skirt, Lacey quickly identified her house key and unlocked the door. She flicked the light switch and a pale-yellow glow filled the living room. "Would you like some lemonade?"

Kendra hooked her arm again and steered her to her white wicker couch with the cactus floral cushions. "No, I don't want anything to drink. I want you to tell me why you and that hunk of a firefighter out there aren't living happily ever after on a ranch in Orson."

Lacey sat and clasped her hands as Kendra pulled the matching wicker chair over to sit opposite her.

"I'm not sure where to start."

"Okay, then I'll ask the questions and you answer them. How long had you two been an item?"

Technically, they had met sophomore year of high school, but it was their junior year that they became an item. "About two years."

"How long has it been since you last saw him?"

She gripped her hands tighter. "Eight years."

"And what caused the breakup?"

Lacey narrowed her eyes. "That stupid arson charge." Her tone dripped with bitterness she couldn't control. She'd always been a good girl, and being accused of something she didn't do had rankled.

"Ah, so he broke up with you because he thought you were a firebug and as a future firefighter he couldn't be with you."

"Yes. No. I mean, yes, he did believe the accusations and dumped me because he couldn't be with 'someone like me' as he so graciously put it. But he was a cowboy then, not a firefighter. He was supposed to stay in Orson and take over his parents' horse ranch."

Kendra pondered that information for a moment. "But didn't you say when I hired you that they ruled that fire as accidental?"

She shrugged. "Yes, but by the time they made that decision, I was away at school and my reputation in Orson was dirt." The fact was, she'd been lucky to escape from the burning carriage house. It had taken her over a year to get over the nightmares of waking up in the dark, her lungs filling with smoke.

Kendra stood. "I want you to stay in this casita all night. I don't want anyone trying to blame this fire on you."

"You believe me?"

Her boss rolled her eyes. "Lacey, I didn't have to work with you for a year and let you handle all my money to know you wouldn't have started a fire. The fact that some idiot who supposedly loved you couldn't figure it out doesn't mean the rest of the world is so stupid."

Tears welled in her eyes and Lacey threw her arms around Kendra. "Thank you."

Her boss gave her a tight hug, then pushed her back. "First rule, don't let him see your weakness. Got it?"

Lacey nodded and brushed her tears away with the hem of her western shirt, even though her heart was breaking all over again. Kendra had been a professional poker player and if anyone would know how to appear to Cole, it would be her.

"Second, don't give him the opportunity to point fingers. Go about your daily business as if nothing unusual has happened."

She nodded. "But what about the real reason the fire started?"

Kendra scowled. "Shit, that could be anything from more vandals hating our nudist business to a careless construction worker to a guest with an arson record. We'll let the fire department figure that out. Okay?"

"Okay." She straightened her shoulders. "I'll stay here tonight and review Selma's inventory. I have it on my computer."

Kendra walked to the door. "Good. Maybe you can also check our reservations and see if anyone is due to arrive tomorrow. I'd like to know what kind of guest relation mitigation we will be up against with the police and fire people here."

"Already did." Lacey opened the door for her boss. "No one is due to check in until Wednesday when Ginger and Buddy arrive, unless we have day guests."

Kendra smiled. "Good. That's one thing in our favor. Ginger and Buddy won't care." Instead of turning away, her boss shifted her weight, a clear sign she was concerned.

Lacey's stomach tightened. "What is it?"

"I just realized how important it is for me to hire a new security guard. It's been so quiet this fall I haven't made time for interviews. Now with your ex in the area, I'm thinking that should become my first priority."

She was about to reassure Kendra that Cole didn't have a dangerous bone in his body, but she swallowed her words as the image of him hefting his fellow firefighters away from the flames came to mind. The teenage Cole certainly didn't have that kind of strength. Truth be told, she didn't know *this* Cole Hatcher at all.

Cole fell into a cushioned chair in the Poker Flat Nudist Resort's lobby and lifted the neck of his t-shirt up to wipe his eyes. The material came away dotted with tiny black specks. Shit, he needed a shower. Just a few more minutes and he could head back to the station.

Wade Johnson, the resort manager, strode away in search of his fiancée, the owner of Poker Flat. The man had stayed up all night with him. Their mutual interest in protecting the horses had Cole thinking. It may be a nudist resort but it was still a resort. He couldn't pass up a possible opportunity for the horses from his and his grandfather's ranch. He'd see if he could get a business card.

Crossing his legs at his ankles, Cole leaned back. He had to admit the resort was first class. The chair he sat in was so comfortable he'd have to be careful not to fall asleep. He glanced at the wooden clock above the receptionist desk. 5:50 a.m. He doubted many nudist guests would be up yet. He could close his eyes until Wade returned. Watching for hot spots all night to protect the desert and the horses had been a strain on the eyes.

A slight change in air temperature was the only warning he had he wasn't alone anymore.

"Oh come on, Selma. You were sitting at your kitchen table twiddling your fingers waiting for the sun to rise. Now you have an extra ten minutes to prep your huevos rancheros."

"Humph. Could have used the extra minutes for my beauty sleep."

Cole opened one eye. Lacey strode toward the front desk in a pair of white cowgirl boots with fringe, a too short white skirt, and a loose white blouse with tiny pink stars and six-shooters printed on it. The only thing missing was a white hat, except she had that too, in her hand. From behind she made him think of a piece of tres leches cake with strawberries on top. The desire to eat her up hit him in the groin.

She stopped at the desk and gave the shorter woman with salt-and-pepper hair a quick hug. "You are far too beautiful as it is."

The woman ducked away, grumbling, but Lacey smiled after her fondly. Cole's heart thumped hard in his chest. He remembered that smile. It had made him believe he could conquer the world. Too bad he hadn't had her with him when he needed to conquer his parents.

Lacey moved to adjust the pamphlets on the side of the counter. Her shapely legs had a slight tan as they disappeared beneath the ass-hugging skirt. He scowled. She shouldn't wear such revealing clothes to work. Was she looking to get laid? Her straight blonde hair was caught in a braid on one side of her neck, giving her an innocent look.

She wasn't innocent at all. As a randy teen, he'd made sure of that. Need slithered through his crotch and up his backbone. The first time he'd had her petite body beneath his own, he'd been afraid of crushing her. But his little lady was made of sterner stuff on the inside. His balls tightened and he shifted in the chair, his erection making him uncomfortable. She'd been so tight.

"What are *you* doing here?"

Cowboy's Match (Poker Flat #2)

Also by Lexi Post

Contemporary Cowboy Romance

Cowboys Never Fold
(Poker Flat Series: Book 1)
Cowboy's Match
(Poker Flat Series: Book 2)
Cowboy's Best Shot
(Poker Flat Series: Book 3)
Cowboy's Break
(Poker Flat Series: Book 4)
Wedding at Poker Flat
(Poker Flat Series: Book 5)

Christmas with Angel
(Poker Flat Series Book 2.5, Last Chance Series: Book 1)
Trace's Trouble
(Last Chance Series: Book 2)
Fletcher's Flame
(Last Chance Series: Book 3)
Logan's Luck
(Last Chance Series: Book 4)

Dillon's Dare
(Last Chance Series: Book 5)
Riley's Rescue
(Last Chance Series: Book 6)

Aloha Cowboy
(Island Cowboy Series: Book 1)

Military Romance

When Love Chimes (Broken Valor Series: Book 1)
Poisoned Honor (Broken Valor Series: Book 2)

Paranormal Romance

Masque
Passion's Poison
Passion of Sleepy Hollow
Heart of Frankenstein

Pleasures of Christmas Past
(A Christmas Carol Series: Book 1)
Desires of Christmas Present
(A Christmas Carol Series: Book 2)
Temptations of Christmas Future
(A Christmas Carol: Book 3)
One of A Kind Christmas
(A Christmas Carol Series: Book 4)

On Highland Time
(Time Weavers, Inc.: Book 1)

A Pocket in Time
(Time Weavers, Inc. Book 2) *Coming in 2020*

Sci-fi Romance

Cruise into Eden
(The Eden Series: Book 1)
Unexpected Eden
(The Eden Series: Book 2)
Eden Discovered
(The Eden Series: Book 3)
Eden Revealed
(The Eden Series: Book 4)
Avenging Eden
(The Eden Series: Book 5)
Beast of Eden
(Eden Series: Book 6)
Bound by Eden
(The Eden Series: Book 7) *Coming Soon*

About Lexi Post

Lexi Post is a New York Times and USA Today best-selling author of romance inspired by the classics. She spent years in higher education taking and teaching courses about the classical literature she loved. From Edgar Allan Poe's short story "The Masque of the Red Death" to Tolstoy's *War and Peace*, she's read, studied, and taught wonderful classics.

But Lexi's first love is romance novels. In an effort to marry her two first loves, she started writing romance inspired by the classics and found she loved it. From hot paranormals to sizzling cowboys to hunks from out of this world, Lexi provides a sensuous experience with a "whole lotta story."

Lexi is living her own happily ever after with her husband and her cat in Florida. She makes her own ice cream every weekend, loves bright colors, and you will never see her without a hat.

www.lexipostbooks.com

Printed in Great Britain
by Amazon

56062915R10136